W9-BUX-072

The Heroine's Bookshelf

The HEROINE'S Bookshelf

Life Lessons from Jane Austen to Laura Ingalls Wilder

ERIN BLAKEMORE

HARPER

An Imprint of HarperCollins*Publishers*
www.harpercollins.com

HarperCollins books may be purchased for educational, business, or sales promotional use. For information, please write: Special Markets Department, HarperCollins Publishers, 10 East 53rd Street, New York, NY 10022.

FIRST EDITION

Designed by Eric Butler

Library of Congress Cataloging-in-Publication Data has been applied for.

ISBN: 978-0-06-195876-2

10 11 12 13 14   OV/RRD   10 9 8 7 6 5 4 3 2 1

For Richard, because I promised.

Death and taxes and childbirth!
There's never any convenient time for any of them!

MARGARET MITCHELL, *GONE WITH THE WIND*

"Whatever comes," she said, "cannot alter one thing.
If I am a princess in rags and tatters, I can be a princess
inside. It would be easy to be a princess if I were dressed
in cloth of gold, but it is a great deal more of a triumph
to be one all the time when no one knows it."

FRANCES HODGSON BURNETT, *A LITTLE PRINCESS*

CONTENTS

INTRODUCTION

In times of struggle, there are as many reasons not to read as there are to breathe. Don't you have better things to do? Reading, let alone *re*reading, is the terrain of milquetoasts and mopey spinsters. At life's ugliest junctures, the very act of opening a book can smack of cowardly escapism. Who chooses to read when there's work to be done?

Call me a coward if you will, but when the line between duty and sanity blurs, you can usually find me curled up with a battered book, reading as if my mental health depended on it. And it does, for inside the books I love I find food, respite, escape, and perspective. I find something else, too: heroines and authors, hundreds of them, women whose real and fictitious lives have covered the terrain I too must tread.

Oh, have I needed some heroines in my life.

I needed them when I was eleven years old and my parents had become strangers, my body was going psycho, and my friends had turned into evil junior-high aliens. I needed them when I was adrift in college, unsure of my place in a new city and among new ideas. I need them now as I stand up to big decisions about family, career, what to eat for breakfast. Fortunately, they've lined up on my bookshelf, patiently waiting for me to read and rediscover their stories. They've been there all along, pegging away at their sewing like Jo March, carrying hods of coal like Sara Crewe, breaking trails through thick snow and bitter circumstance like Laura Ingalls. Some were conceived of two hundred years ago, but the track marks they left on the road are surprisingly fresh. They've been there for me through everything adolescence and adulthood have lobbed my way. They're there for you, too, should you choose to acknowledge them.

I'm not the only person I know who condescends to dive into "mere children's literature" (as some have called it) when called to face down adulthood. In winter 2008, as I contemplated my favorite heroines' takes on financial hardship in the face of a crushing recession, I started to talk to my friends about reading, even the ones who long ago traded screens for pages and BlackBerries for actual conversations. Reading, it seemed, was catching. All at once we were feverishly revisiting books we had neglected for years. Snowbound, edgy, kept inside by colds and coughs and frugality, we turned toward known literary quantities. And the familiar women we found pressed inside the covers—Anne Shirley, Jane Eyre, Scout Finch—had much to add to stories we already knew backward and forward and lessons to impart that may have eluded us when we read them in earlier years. Reading and rereading became a system of emotional mile markers, a "you are here" to reference as we prepared to travel heroines' paths.

These paths were not easy ones. As women, we are the protagonists of our own personal novels. We are called upon to be the heroines of our own lives, not supporting characters. We wake up with tasks to do. Sometimes they're mundane—Pa wants us to stomp down some hay before the winter comes. Sometimes they're ugly—it's time to walk away from the man who conveniently neglected to inform us of that woman he's had locked up in the attic for the past decade. Sometimes they're scary—a sister lies on her deathbed as a father struggles in a distant hospital.

If you're anything like me, you'll falter and balk at these tasks, these markers of a heroine's path. Luckily, we're not required to be brave to be heroines . . . all we have to do is show up for our own stories. Even if the reality is less glamorous than fiction (my inner heroine, for example, sometimes struggles to change out of her workout clothes or make her bed like a grown-up), even when it feels impossible to tap into a spirit that's bigger and better than you, but IS you, we're called upon to lead big, sloppy, frustrating lives.

Luckily, the road ahead has been traveled before, trudged through by heroines with singed hems and snow-clotted boots. Our favorite authors and their plucky protagonists have much to teach in times of strife, even when our own heroic spirits have been dampened and deflated. A bit of literary intervention can give your inner heroine the guts she needs to keep pedaling when the entire concept of fitness seems daunting, to confront a disrespectful supervisor or survive formative and miserable life crucibles like childbirth or end-of-life care. Literary heroines face things like judgmental neighbors and bumbling proposals of marriage with aplomb. And they were given these qualities by women writers, some long-dead, real women with bills to pay, relatives to appease, children to feed and educate, and selves to discover. Just like you.

Wait, you say. The kids are crying, the phone is ringing, and I'm dead tired from putting in my hour on the elliptical. My mom has cancer, and I've got a headache; what if it's a tumor? I can't handle being asked to do one more thing, ever. Surely I have nothing to give to a book. And a book can't possibly have anything to give to me.

I am here to posit that it's exactly in these moments of struggle and stress that we need books the most. There's something in the pause to read that's soothing in and of itself. A moment with a book is basic self-care, the kind of skill you pass along to your children as you would a security blanket or a churchgoing habit. It's a pair of glasses you let sit on your nose for a few stolen hours, coloring your familiar living room and the blustery world outside with the lens of another woman's experience. It's a familiar book, rediscovered and dusted off, cracked open at random until you're sucked in again. It reads differently at different junctures in your life, but that's part of the fun. Time travel, redemption, escape, and self-knowledge are all neatly bound and sewn into the modest covers of the books we pass from hand to hand, library to purse, mother to daughter, where heroines' lessons live long after they've gone out of print or disintegrated from love and wear.

As an inveterate, useless, cranky, committed, and unabashed bookworm, I've had ample opportunity to call on the lives of the heroines as I negotiate my own path. At the darkest times of my life, I've turned to the books that are my oxygen. I was a freaky, hyperactive, and hyperbolic child, a kid who needed more friends than she was dealt. And I found them pressed into the pages of lopsided library books and the cheaply bound novels I hoarded my allowance to buy at the school book fair. I read standing up and lying down, in secret and during loud public gatherings. Others obsessed about painting their toenails in two strokes instead of three or spent their time teasing their bangs into the perfect late 1980s fall-with-pouf. Meanwhile, I laced up my inner corset and tackled the harsh world of unforgiving moors and unrelenting stepmothers.

My literary companions would never live in the ranch house with the atrocious rust-red carpet my parents couldn't afford to replace, but no matter. They accompanied me to my first kiss and my first breakup, through college and into the weird uncharted territory of quarterlife crisis and grown womanhood. Somehow, painfully, I came closer to myself with every book I read, even—especially—the ones that took place in far-off and inaccessible lands.

This wasn't as much about becoming a cliché or a walking ad for libraries as it was about getting through my life. And it still is—only now I know I wasn't the only one with a parallel existence led while sitting on schoolbuses and airplanes or standing in line at the post office. I was accompanied by thousands, millions, of other girls and women like me, the women who join me and these heroines and authors daily. These heroines had much to teach when we were girls bursting out of ourselves, and they have even more to offer the women we've become: would-be heroines with the inconvenient mission of facing everything a protagonist's path has in store.

Reading books used to be just as transgressive as writing them. After all, good books sow the seeds of future actions. They feed us when we get divorced, walk out on jobs or unequal relationships, raise uppity daughters, and demand our due. They comfort us when we're lonely and give us the words we crave. Don't we owe the women who dared to provide them a bit of our undivided attention?

Two hundred years ago, the mothers of the books we take for granted were lumped together in the same lowly category as factory workers, governesses, and prostitutes. A respectable woman didn't write, she took care of her household: if she were rich, she oversaw a staff of servants and entertained for a living; if she were poor, she carried out endless labors punctuated by births and deaths. Jane Austen had to publish her books anonymously at a time when women were lucky to be taught to read. Louisa May

Alcott and Charlotte Brontë both published under male pseudonyms, their writing the only vent for their active minds. Even Margaret Mitchell was the subject of scandal and derision in the twentieth century for her decision to pursue a newswoman's career. Like their heroines, these women writers had much to endure. Some wrote against incredible odds or in secret; others faced down prejudice or poverty in their pursuit of a better life.

When I started looking into the stories of the authors who mean so much to me, I didn't know I was in for a few shocks. I can't be the only person who was initially disheartened to learn that *Little Women* was a labor of practicality, not love, for Louisa May Alcott. Written in mere weeks and considered lesser literature by Alcott herself, it was quickly finished and even more quickly turned into groceries and clothing for her struggling family. Frances Hodgson Burnett was just as famous for her inappropriate affairs as her timeless children's books; Margaret Mitchell was almost barred from polite society for her wild behavior. How dare I enjoy, even learn from, the fruits of these female authors, especially the books I now know to be distractions from adult literary careers and happy lives, written under duress and in grave emotional pain?

But even if Alcott meant not a word of her most beloved

book, its pages contain the truths I need to face the horrors of being a restless worker and a disappointing daughter. Sure, it's moralizing and artificially cheerful, but the power of its message is underscored by its author's story. Embedded inside the books I love, even those written by unwilling hands, are the stories of women's struggles to survive, to define themselves as authors and as human beings whose worth went beyond a paycheck or a byline. These heroines' messages couldn't exist without the strife from which they were written, and the power of each story is magnified by the triumphs and failures that followed. Knowing the rest of the story deepens the act of reading itself.

Writing a book about reading at a time when the practical is the popular has been a rare challenge. Surely there's always something better to do than revisit women who've been dead for centuries. As I wrote this book, I reread my childhood favorites and encountered new voices and stories, supplementing the books themselves with a rich selection of biographies and archival materials. In the course of its composition, I've moved from awe (total absorption in story and narrative) to obsession (the fun stage in which I read lengthy descriptions of a debutante year or make up my *Little Women* name) to guilt (who am I, a writer assisted by Diet Coke and Google and inexpensive transcontinental communications, to even pick up a book written with a quill pen before a wood fire?). After a while, even my breaks fed the book, every pause bringing a reminder of the enduring quality of "my" heroines and authors, from the distinctly Scarlett-like charm of a youth-obsessed Madonna to familiar notes of Frances Hodgson Burnett in the downfall and deaths of celebrities like Farrah Fawcett, Michael Jackson, and Brittany Murphy.

As I befriended the women behind the books, I was reminded that they were as human as any modern woman. Louisa May Alcott? Testy morphine addict. Betty Smith? Chain-smoker with a terrible knack for picking the wrong men. Like their heroines, the women behind some of literature's most important and enduring books weren't perfect. Most of them didn't even come close: their lives were pocked by acrimony and despair, family feuds and miserable, boring jobs. They showed up for them anyway. The heroism of these authors lies not in the perfection of their pursuits, but in the fact that they bequeathed us something in the process, something that came from the stumbling-through and survival that is our collective lot.

I may not write with a blotty fountain pen or a typewriter; I may never change the world. But I feel a wild closeness to the Lucy Maud Montgomeries and Zora Neale Hurstons who left us their life stories. These were women who could chop wood and tell off nasty critics, women with the guts and the tenacity to write when they lacked power, heat, and health. Over the past months they've become my fast friends, not just because they've given me a glimpse into the heroic life but because they've revealed a tiny bit of my own potential in the process.

In times of struggle, there are as many reasons not to read as there are to breathe. Accompanied by the heroines on my bookshelf, I choose to do both.

The Heroine's Bookshelf

CHAPTER 1

SELF

Lizzy Bennet in *Pride and Prejudice,* by Jane Austen

What wild imaginations one forms where dear self is concerned! How sure to be mistaken!

JANE AUSTEN, *PERSUASION*

It is a truth universally acknowledged that going back on a proposal of marriage isn't the best way to start the day. Jane broke the news over breakfast, then begged for a carriage to deliver her safely back to her family home in Bath. Her hostesses' adieus were icy at best, in sad contrast to the pleasure with which their family had greeted her. It was a predicament, well, fit for a Jane Austen heroine, only this time the heroine was the author herself. She couldn't afford not to marry. So why was she speeding away from Manydown Park as fast as her borrowed carriage could carry her, fleeing the only proposal she had ever received?

The author of *Pride and Prejudice* and *Emma* wasn't exactly known for her romantic conquests, and the twenty-seven-year-old had already prepared herself for a spinster's fate. It wasn't that she was unattractive; indeed, her charms were fresh enough for any Regency drawing room. She had even managed to attract a romantic scandal years before. Still, things just hadn't gelled, and it began to seem as if she'd be a dependent relative forever.

Back in her prime at age twenty-one, financial worries hadn't seemed real to spirited Jane, who possessed an unusually broad education in addition to a lady's expected accomplishments in drawing, dancing, and penmanship. Her penchant for conversation and her playful wit attracted the attention of Tom Lefroy, a young Irishman who went public with his admiration. Jane reveled in Tom's conversation, tinged with an Irish accent. The couple conversed publicly, met in friends' homes, and danced enough to incite juicy speculation. "I am almost afraid to tell you how my Irish friend and I behaved," she wrote to her sister in 1796. "Imagine to yourself everything most profligate and shocking in the way of dancing and sitting down together."

Though her references to Tom were lighthearted, Jane

couldn't hide her attraction. Tom was everywhere: for months, he occupied her ballroom, her living room, and her blithe letters. By the time he returned to Ireland to study law, Jane considered herself engaged in heart, if not in fact.

Preoccupied, but energized, she threw herself into her work, completing her first two novels (*Sense and Sensibility* and *Pride and Prejudice*) before realizing that Tom wasn't coming back. She never found out why her Irish love fell out of contact, but she suspected it had something to do with her poverty. Discouraged from his relationship with Jane by family members, he suddenly announced his engagement to a wealthy woman. Her marriage prospects dashed, Jane got down to the business of being a spinster. She took to wearing dowdy caps and retired from society, committed only to herself and her family, relegated to eternal dependence on her successful brothers, and caught somewhere between marriage market and matronhood.

So six years later, Harris Bigg-Wither's proposal seemed like her out. Jane was a welcome addition to the Bigg-Wither circle at Manydown Park. She accepted the invitation to visit gladly, all too eager to escape her family's home in loathsome Bath and spend time with Alethea and Catherine, Harris's sisters and her intimate friends, in Steventon. And her happy holiday hinted at a permanent vacation: just a week after her arrival, she impulsively accepted Harris's proposal, celebrating her engagement along with her future in-laws. It was only later that night, alone in her bedchamber, that she began to have her doubts.

The decision should have been simple. Her fiancé was eligible, well connected; his hand would mean the difference between financial security and poor-relative status. Marrying Harris wouldn't just make Jane a wife: it would make her a wealthy woman, free of uncomfortable family obligations and the specter of poverty that had haunted her entire adult life.

Still, something about Harris just didn't sit well with Jane. He was nearly six years her junior, an awkward, hulking young man with a distasteful stutter and a notorious temper. And though she had known him since childhood, nothing about his physical stature or gauche behavior had managed to endear him to her. Harris had family and fortune to recommend him, but was Jane's friendship with his sisters enough to justify a loveless marriage?

Jane knew this was probably her last chance at a life as the wife of a respectable man. But it was an opportunity she could not take in good conscience: the next morning she broke off her engagement in a mixture of disgrace, relief, and resolve.

No diaries or correspondence recording Jane's thoughts on her choice survive, but it's no coincidence that most of her novels deal with the difficulty and rarity of mutual love. Later in life, Jane wrote to her niece, advising her to marry for love and love alone. "Having written so much on one side of the question," she wrote, "I shall turn round & entreat you not to commit yourself farther, & not to think of accepting him unless you really do like him. Anything is to be preferred or endured rather than marrying without Affection."

Jane's choice to end her embarrassing engagement was the first foray into the battle for self-definition she would fight for the rest of her life. An outsider by choice, Jane developed a keen sense of observation and sarcasm. She was drawn to parody and self-deprecation, absorbed by the absurd. And what better place to hone her talent than on the drawing-room scandals and small-town romances that surrounded her?

Though she wrote the book that would become *Pride and Prejudice* eight years before she cemented her single status forever, you wouldn't know it to read it. Jane must have foreseen her own heroine's journey toward self-reliance when she took to her pen in 1796, for her most famous book contains not one but two rejected suitors—and a heroine whose sense of self is rivaled only by her creator's.

Modern women aren't called upon to attach themselves to the first eligible man who shows his face, but that won't keep them from seeing themselves in the book's heroine. Elizabeth Bennet is vital, naughty, saucy, smart. And like her creator, she's not about to sacrifice herself on the altar of a loveless life. Even in the company of other memorable Austen heroines like worldly Emma Woodhouse or wicked Mary Crawford, Lizzy more than holds her own. Her specialty? Poking holes in the ridiculous. Her cross to bear? A marriage-obsessed family with no money to support its five daughters.

Lizzy's world is as uptight and constrained as a Regency-era dance, but this heroine isn't exactly resigned to her fate. She's happy to cooperate with the social niceties, but when it comes to major life decisions, she knows herself far too well to be taken in by mere words, formalities, or expectations. And nowhere is Lizzy's raucous, flawed, and decided sense of self more clear or more enticing than in the moments in which she does exactly the opposite of what she is expected to do. When called upon to sit languid in some living room, Lizzy heads out for a bit of exercise in the muddy fields that surround Meryton. When presented with Wickham, a man of few credentials and many charms, she lets her true feelings show. Provoked by her wild sisters, she remains indifferent and ineffably calm. And when proposed to by the wrong man, she refuses to play along.

By all unimaginative calculations, bumbling Mr. Collins is the perfect match for Lizzy. After all, he holds the keys to the Bennet property, has a doting patroness, and is more than willing to share his estate in exchange for a fetching wife. But by a heroine's standards, Mr. Collins is just not going to happen. He's unattractive, pedantic, stifling . . . everything a self-respecting heroine must avoid. To her mother's chagrin, Lizzy runs the other way, roundly rejecting Collins and refusing to place money before love. When her friend Charlotte Lucas accepts Collins instead, Lizzy gives vent to her true feelings:

> "To oblige you, I would try to believe almost anything, but no one else could be benefited by such a belief as this; for were I persuaded that Charlotte had any regard for him, I should only think worse of her understanding than I now do of her heart. My dear Jane, Mr. Collins is a conceited, pompous, narrow-minded, silly man; you know he is, as well as I do; and you must feel, as well as I do, that the woman who marries him cannot have a proper way of thinking."

Lizzie's sense of self doesn't just point her in the right direction, it prevents her from going down a dangerous path. We're left feeling sorry for Charlotte, but we can't exactly nod our heads in approval as Lizzie's friend thumbs her nose at a heroine's promise. By marrying a man so far beneath her, Charlotte has relegated herself forever to the annals of supporting characters. For any real heroine, Collins is the equivalent of literary kryptonite.

Okay, so it's easy, even expected, for Lizzy to turn down Mr. Collins. But what about when the man making an offer is proud, conceited Fitzwilliam Darcy? Though Darcy has been introduced as diffident and self-absorbed, we can't help but root for him a little. After all, preoccupied Lizzy has allowed her preconceived notions to mask his growing interest. Too absorbed in her dislike of him to acknowledge their complex flirtation, Lizzy doesn't see Darcy for who he is. We don't have that problem: though Jane doesn't favor us with a full description, it's hard to picture him as anything but brutally hot, staggeringly wealthy, and intelligent enough to really appreciate Lizzy despite his serious misgivings about her family.

It is these doubts, honestly but uncouthly stated, that trigger one of literature's most withering marital rejections. Lizzy's floored when Darcy suddenly asks for her hand, but we've been better prepared. Still, we cringe right along with her as Darcy lays down a proposal so backhanded it comes right around to slap him in the face. Her vanity insulted and any chance of romantic communion ground into dust under Darcy's riding boots, Lizzy thinks fast. And self prevails:

"You are mistaken, Mr. Darcy, if you suppose that the mode of your declaration affected me in any other way, than as it spared the concern which I might have felt in refusing you, had you behaved in a more gentlemanlike manner."

She saw him start at this, but he said nothing, and she continued:

"You could not have made the offer of your hand in any possible way that would have tempted me to accept it."

Again his astonishment was obvious; and he looked at her with an expression of mingled incredulity and mortification. She went on:

"From the very beginning—from the first moment, I may almost say—of my acquaintance with you, your manners, impressing me with the fullest belief of your arrogance, your conceit, and your selfish disdain of the feelings of others, were such as to form the groundwork of disapprobation on which succeeding events have built so immovable a dislike; and I had not known you a month before I felt that you were the last man in the world whom I could ever be prevailed on to marry."

Lizzy's split-second decision is true to her heroine's self, a self that won't be trodden upon by any arrogant man. Darcy's not just due for a refusal—his insulting proposal means he's the last man in the world she'd ever accept. Overcome by embarrassment and outrage, Lizzy flings both caution and future aside with a few choice words. For a heroine, anything would do but to marry a man she can neither love nor respect.

But heroines are human, too, and we're along for the comedown that overtakes Lizzy once she has time to think over her refusal (Darcy's impassioned letter, which explains his behavior and casts doubt on Wickham's true nature, doesn't hurt, either). A waffling Lizzy is even better than decisive, spirited Lizzy precisely because her questions and doubts are so real. Was her ballsy refusal actually a terrible mistake? Will Darcy ever forgive her impulsive, hurtful words? Can a man with a gorgeous estate like Pemberley be all bad? Any woman who's ever stayed up at night reliving an important conversation or planning out a difficult one can identify with Lizzy's plight.

> She grew absolutely ashamed of herself. Of neither Darcy nor Wickham could she think without feeling she had been blind, partial, prejudiced, absurd.
>
> "How despicably I have acted!" she cried; "I, who have prided myself on my discernment! . . . Pleased with the preference of one, and offended by the neglect of the other, on the very beginning of our acquaintance, I have courted prepossession and ignorance, and driven reason away, where either were concerned. Till this moment I never knew myself."

It would be all too easy for Lizzy to mope and resign herself to her pride's spectacular fall, but Lizzy is a heroine of action. Ever on the hunt for self-understanding, she is forced to evaluate her own role in the debacle, and what she sees is not flattering. Given the chance to behave heroically, Lizzy shines: in the face of her own shortcomings, she doesn't flinch for a second. Instead, she confronts herself with a heroine's daring. It's time to change and challenge the beliefs she once held so dear.

With new self-knowledge comes new resolve, and Lizzy

softens toward Darcy when they unexpectedly meet in Derbyshire. It isn't long before she must acknowledge that their relationship goes far beyond cold mutual acquaintance—knowledge that helps her stand up to a bullying aunt and dare to declare her own truth. Tellingly, love doesn't hit Lizzy until she's open enough to receive as well as give it. And what she does get will inspire a tiny spark of jealousy in anyone but the most angelic reader.

The heart of *Pride and Prejudice* is more than a love story—it's a heroine's fearless confrontation of herself, complete with family humiliations and fatal flaws. Jane isn't easy on Lizzy: she draws her literary daughter with just as many shortcomings as strengths. Her worst traits are brought to the fore by her inane parents and absurd sisters, people who encourage her to be petty and dismissive, and to laugh away her troubles. No, Lizzy's not perfect, and her prejudices are as much a part of herself as the bravado that leads her to walk three miles in the mud to visit her ill sister or contradict pompous Lady Catherine de Bourgh in defense of herself and her love. Lizzy and Darcy must both embrace each other's entire selves if they are to get their happy ending. First, though, both must look within.

Jane Austen knew all too well that self is elusive and everchanging. After all, she specialized in sudden realizations and blemished but self-determined heroines. Throughout *Pride and Prejudice*, she urges us to take an honest look at ourselves and, more importantly, to face what we see with a heroine's bravado. Does that fearlessness mean we can't succumb to (or laugh at) our woes? No way: the laughter and the doubts are part of the heroine's journey toward a more complete self.

Like her most famous heroine, Jane Austen never really came to terms with a society that expected her to repress her true opinions and strengths in favor of frivolous "accomplishments." Contrary to popular perceptions (and her fans' desires), she tended toward Darcy-like discontent, spending much of her adult life carving out a unique space for her dissatisfied self. We lucked out when Jane decided to take a pass on a mundane life full of fancy work and frills, daring instead to act on behalf of her real passions. And we're lucky that she passed some of that fire—and courage—to her literary daughter.

Lizzy, like Jane, knows full well that turning down Darcy and the ridiculous Collins means she may never marry. She does it anyway. Even if Lizzy didn't get her happy ending, we get the feeling that she would have been happy all the same, content in a position much like the one her creator occupied. "Till I have your disposition, your goodness, I never can have your happiness," she tells her sister Jane. "No, no, let me shift for myself; and, perhaps, if I have very good luck, I may meet with another Mr. Collins in time." Though everyone around her is intent on freaking out around love and marriage, Lizzy doesn't have to play along. Self-assured and self-respecting, she doesn't need a man to complete her, even if she gets one in the end. And we can't help but suspect that she'll find plenty of laughter in life, married or not.

Jane Austen's decision not to marry meant giving up the possibility of the romantic happy ending she invariably gave her heroines, but it didn't mean giving up her enjoyment of life. A novelist at a time when true ladies never sought public regard, Jane dared to envision a life defined by professional accomplishments rather than personal connections. As a writer and a woman, she forged a life that reflected the deepest callings of a heroine's self—laughing at polite society, poking fun, never conforming completely to the model of a mannered woman. It was something that placed her at odds with expectation even as it fed her innermost self. But losing the approbation of others for her own self's sake was a risk Jane was more than willing to take.

Two hundred years after Jane Austen dared to be herself, a modern heroine's got to shore up her resources. Circumstance and romance change constantly, but there's something to be said for leaning into what you know. If "self" isn't part of that arsenal, what's the point of the struggle? Self is what we fight for, where we come from. Flawed or not (and what heroine is not flawed?), we're the only constant in our lives. Often, our selves are the only place we have to come back to. The landscape is weird and ever-changing, but it's one well worth getting to know.

Luckily, no heroine is called upon to know herself at all times. In fact, Lizzy proves that blind adherence to prejudices and principles is its own kind of folly. Think of the boredom of a *Pride and Prejudice* in which neither quality was challenged, changed, or overcome. Lizzy's imperfection is also her appeal, and ours. Thankfully, we're allowed to get some mud on our petticoats, change our minds, even turn down a Darcy once in a while, as long as we come back to ourselves in the end. Change is inherent in "self," but one thing should never change: our commitment to whichever self we possess right now. Staking a claim to self may be scary, but it's always necessary.

It's easy to dismiss a two-hundred-year-old book as a literary chestnut, a historical oddity that couldn't possibly apply to modern life. But hemlines shift far more quickly than human nature, and Jane's story of romantic confusion and changing opinions is just as vital and funny as it must have been for its first readers. Jane Austen's witty heroines have pervaded every level of culture, from *Clueless* to chick lit, and her influence isn't going anywhere anytime soon. There's certainly no dust on my copy of *Pride and Prejudice*, for the book remains relevant no matter where I find myself. My life is more concerned with career politics than marital ones, but that doesn't keep me from finding Lizzy's spirit wherever authority is flouted, minds changed, and expectations challenged.

Looking for a modern-day Lizzy? Seek out the people with enough perspective to laugh their way through the crappy and the ridiculous. I channel my inner Lizzy whenever I bump up against absurd expectations or laughable characters (surely I have a Lizzy-like disregard of self-important lawyers to thank for getting me through my paralegal years). Like Miss Bennet, I am called upon to examine my own actions, change what I don't like, and adhere to my gut instincts. Like Miss Austen, I am called upon to create my own place in life, one that is true to the person I am and not the person anyone else expects me to be. It isn't easy to answer this call, but I know I'm in good company whenever I do. And every time I revisit *Pride and Prejudice*, I am reminded that when dealt a hand of Collinses and Wickhams, indecision and regret, there really isn't any acceptable substitute for my own boisterous, uncertain self.

READ THIS BOOK:

- When your mom complains that you'll never give her grandchildren
- When your inner people-pleaser threatens to drown out your gut instinct
- As an antidote to deathly seriousness

LIZZY'S LITERARY SISTERS:

- Emma Woodhouse in *Emma*, by Jane Austen
- Bridget Jones in *Bridget Jones's Diary*, by Helen Fielding
- Hermione Granger in J. K. Rowling's Harry Potter series

CHAPTER 2

FAITH

Janie Crawford in *Their Eyes Were Watching God*, by Zora Neale Hurston

Faith hasn't got no eyes, but she's long-legged

But take de spy-glass of Faith

And look into dat upper room

When you are alone to yourself

When yo' heart is burnt with fire, ha!

REVEREND C. C. LOVELACE,

AS TRANSCRIBED BY ZORA NEALE HURSTON

Years later, she'd clock a man with her pocketbook and step over his unconscious body on the way to a rent party. She'd sweat out her bruises and blessings in a mysterious Haitian voodoo ritual. But in 1917, there was no glimpse of the woman who'd write *Their Eyes Were Watching God* or become a keen cultural anthropologist with a "burning bush inside." At the time, Zora Neale Hurston was just a young woman who made a bet with God.

Twenty-six-year-old Zora was anything but heroic as she lay in her hospital bed. She felt sick and scared, downed by appendicitis and with no family or friends to visit or console her. It had been many years since she sat with her father on the sweltering porches of Eatonville, Florida, listening to her elders weave long yarns about their all-black community and its history. Back then, she was curious and spunky, reveling in her place in a respected preacher's family. That was before her mother died and her father—a strict man, notoriously intolerant of other people's frailties—turned into a stranger.

Something about Zora just rubbed John Hurston the wrong way. A religious man, he was anything but perfect, an infamous womanizer who internalized the hatred he had experienced at the hands of the white community before he helped found Eatonville. His blatant favoritism for her brothers and his clumsy mistreatment of the daughter who resembled him most was a brutal emotional blow for openhearted Zora. And his behavior after the death of her mother, Lucy Ann Hurston, was just the beginning of a long sequence of insults. Zora soon found herself banished to a school in Jacksonville, then abandoned there at the end of the school year by a father who, irritated by his daughter's incessant needs and angered by her rejection of his new wife, refused to take responsibility for Zora's welfare or tuition. His suggestion that the school just adopt her was a betrayal in the strictest sense of the word.

Still just a teen when she was dumped at school, Zora became an uneasy outcast. In a world that was brutal to black women, she had to depend on relatives and friends for support. Her life from then on out was dark, nomadic, marked by sexual assaults by her white employers, a cruel encounter with her stepmother, and a mysterious relationship she would hint at but never discuss in later years. She was working as a waitress in Baltimore when appendicitis threatened to abbreviate her already troubled life. Too poor to pay for her own treatment, Zora had to rely on the free ward of the Maryland General Hospital for care. She knew that appendicitis was a common killer, one that required swift surgery and a long recovery period—if she lived. Would she die under the knife? Had she fulfilled her purpose here on Earth?

Though stoic about the possibility of death, Zora knew she wasn't ready to go. And so she made a wager that would reverberate throughout the rest of her life. Later she told it so: "I bet God that if I lived, I would try to find out the vague directions whispered in my ears and find the road it seemed I must follow." Zora survived her operation and set out to fulfill her part of the bargain.

She made good on her promise. After a brief stint at Howard University in Washington, D.C., she took Harlem by storm, finding herself right at home in the jazzy, juicy renaissance that filled the neighborhood's literary salons and rent parties in the wild 1920s. Flashy and fiercely attractive, she balanced her writing and her studies with plenty of parties and escapades. She enrolled as the only black student at Barnard College in 1925, and there she finally heard the "vague directions" she had prayed for at the hospital. For the first time, Zora realized that she could translate her interest in black vernacular culture and spiritual traditions into an actual profession. She became a cultural anthropologist, receiving her bachelor's in anthropology at the age of thirty-six.

With superstitions and storytelling her new stock-in-trade, Zora gave in to her new obsession. On fire with the realization that "that man in the gutter is the god-maker," she began to study black religious expression. What she found convinced her that the lowliest of blacks were at the heart of a rich cultural tradition that had never been fully appreciated. Her studies were over for now, but she still had much to learn. For all her enthusiasm, though, Zora wasn't exactly prepared for the depth and breadth of black expression she found back home. As the prodigal daughter turned folklorist returned to the South in 1927 along with her friend Langston Hughes, she tried to make sense of the complex world of folk religion. But she wasn't satisfied with merely transcribing sermons or interviewing preachers. In a break with the traditional anthropological stance of distance, Zora threw herself headfirst into the voodoo, conjuring, and hoodoo traditions of the black South. Soon, she was neck-deep in a strange world of dark traditions, charismatic conjurers, and mysterious rites. She began to collect experiences in addition to notes, training with the South's most respected conjure doctors and undergoing her own spiritual experiences, including a multiday fast whose psychic visions and hallucinations were her fiery initiation into the world of the trained hoodoo practitioner.

Aflame with the power of these spiritual journeys, Zora became convinced that her calling was to convey the drama and sweep of black spirituality for all to see. Though she trained as a priest of sorts, she was no preacher: she was a witness, a disciple, a seeker driven to capture her inner vision in words. She was forty-six years old when she gave that vocation its most powerful expression, writing *Their Eyes Were Watching God* in just seven weeks in 1937 while studying voodoo in Haiti.

Their Eyes Were Watching God is Zora's tour de force, a testament to the external and internal beliefs that drive a heroine to transcend herself and survive everything that God and the elements throw her way. The book follows Janie Crawford, a woman who learns early on that God will do things in his own way and his own good time. As much a volume on faith as a rumination on personal power, self-worth, and love, *Their Eyes Were Watching God* embodies Zora's own personal struggle with her beliefs as it follows Janie's attempts to define and assert her inner strength. And it does so by focusing on a woman who, by 1930s Southern standards, is the least deserving of a powerful spiritual experience.

Throughout the course of the book, we watch Janie survive marriages to a callous man, an attractive tyrant, and a loving younger husband. Abused, ignored, and silenced, Janie is tested again and again. Her liberation from the expectations and judgments of other humans is painfully slow, but powerful. Throughout, she puts her trust in herself and a power greater than herself. The quiet self-confidence that emerges is her tribute to God. Janie draws experience and faith together when she finally speaks up against her husband after decades of stoic silence.

Janie did what she had never done before, that is, thrust herself into the conversation.

"Sometimes God gits familiar wid us womenfolks too and talks His inside business. He told me how surprised He was 'bout y'all turning out so smart after Him makin' yuh different; and how surprised y'all is goin' tuh be if you ever find out you don't know half as much 'bout us as you think you do. It's so easy to make yo'self out God Almighty when you ain't got nothin' tuh strain against but women and chickens."

After you get done cheering, consider that Janie isn't just speaking for herself . . . she's speaking up for a woman's place in God's world. Over the course of the book, Janie settles into that place for good. Women and blacks, too, are God's creations, and criticizing them in God's name just won't fly for Janie (or for Zora). Again and again, Janie watches frail humans fail to do God's work. A neighbor reveals her obsession with light skin and her internalized hatred of the black race in a hubris-ridden parody of God's eternal judgment. Janie is mocked for her love affair with Tea Cake, the man she's waited for all her life. And over and over again, she must look within for answers.

Marked by external strife, Janie's inner life becomes increasingly peaceful as she suspects, then believes, that there's something bigger out there. Though she faces death, emotional starvation, even a hurricane, Janie's hard-won happiness is never really in danger, for she's found redemption and resurrection on the inside. Every facet of Janie's world, both ugly and joyful, is of God's making and God's own goodness; even the terror of the coming storm is made and governed by God. Janie learns that struggling against God's ways is for the weak and confused; for Janie, nothing works but the embrace. For those whose "eyes are watching God," acceptance of the world on the universe's terms is the only thing that can lead to peace. Slowly, mysteriously, God restores all that has been lost. Even God-watchers, though, can't always make sense of divine acts, and a bit of uncertainty and questioning make its way into the book's final affirming passages:

The day of the gun, and the bloody body, and the courthouse came and commenced to sing a sobbing sigh out of every corner in the room; out of each and

every chair and thing. Commenced to sing, commenced to sob and sigh, singing and sobbing. . . .
Here was peace. She pulled in her horizon like a great
fish-net. Pulled it from around the waist of the world
and draped it over her shoulder. So much of life in its
meshes! She called in her soul to come and see.

Janie will always continue her quest for love and self-
definition, whether she's ready to walk down the road or
not. Alone again, she must face some terrifying questions:
Who am I? Who is God? What's the point of faith? Does
God even care? Why must we start over and over, transcend
ourselves again and again?

Like Janie, Zora had reason to question God in the years
following the publication of her now-indelible classic. She
needed all the faith she could muster to face the years that
awaited her. Her growing literary fame and colorful per-
sona had their price. In 1948, she was not only accused of
molesting three boys but was the victim of a brutal slander
campaign by an unrelated party whom she had met only
once. The claims were entirely fabricated—Zora was in
Honduras at the time of the alleged attacks—but it took
six months to acquit herself, and the rest of her life to overcome the effect of the attacks. Though Zora prevailed in

court and all charges were dropped, the rumors surrounding this incident just wouldn't die with the case. Her tattered reputation never managed to recover. Exhausted by a legal battle that had become so cruelly personal, Zora struggled to bounce back.

Zora lived out the last years of her life in almost complete obscurity, fading into forgotten territory along with other lights of the Harlem Renaissance. Overshadowed by new modes of expression, she was mocked for her dramatic, dialect-focused writing style. Her name was entirely neglected by the 1950s, her powerful books long out of print. Plagued by failing health and uncertain finances, she focused instead on her spiritual search as she worked as a substitute teacher and even a maid. But time did not rectify her financial position or mend her fragile health. Tragically, her former friends had almost totally abandoned her by the time she died in 1960. She didn't leave anything behind, not even money enough to be buried in a marked grave.

She may have died impoverished and irrelevant, but Zora's faith in herself and her God brought forth great things during her lifetime. By fusing her talent with a restless spiritual quest, she was able to document and further the beauty her God had made. She took that old bet with

God one step further, translating the sights she saw and the sounds she heard into a powerful vernacular.

Ironically, Zora's choice of self-expression—the dialect of the people for whom she fought so hard professionally and personally—was criticized, even mocked, in her own day. But the last thirty years have revived her reputation, thanks in part to the relentless efforts of Alice Walker, another dialect-driven woman writer whose work has changed the face of American literature. Back in print and deserving of a place on any modern heroine's bookshelf, *Their Eyes Were Watching God* was made into a TV movie produced and hosted by Oprah Winfrey and has been read by countless students. It's a book that was written to be reread and constantly rediscovered, interpreted through the lens of our own diverse spiritual experiences. And it lost none of its power as it traveled from popularity to unsung obscurity and back again. "There is no book as important to me as this one," wrote Alice Walker. "There is enough self-love in that one book—love of community, culture, traditions—to restore a world. Or create a new one."

Fraught with meaning and laden with doubt and emotion, faith and spirituality can be touchy topics for even the bravest heroine. Some leap straight into the fire, eager to find themselves in the flames. Others dance around faith, play with it for a moment before dropping it with scorched fingers. But whether the road to spiritual fulfillment is one of religious belief or strong inner conviction, it's one each heroine must travel, be its result faith, atheism, or something in between.

Janie's trials would bring down a stronger woman with nothing to believe in. Part of the reason her story has remained raw, compelling, is that she *doesn't* have all the answers. When faced with the full force of God's wrath, Janie questions, reconsiders, uncovers something inside of her that's as elemental as a hurricane. Her faith in herself is as strong as her faith in God, and she couldn't withstand what she has to endure without both. But Zora doesn't just leave us with questions: she shows the answers, too, in an ending that is mournful and lonely and comforting all at once. *Their Eyes Were Watching God* finishes with reassurance, but also with a challenge to honor the world in all its beauty and confusion, to draw it as close to us as we dare, to sit with its power even as we face down our own questions about faith.

Not that the questions ever really subside—I for one am a woman whose spirituality is as much about doubt as conviction. But even I find relief and comfort in Janie's steadfast search for the truth, her willingness to face even a hurricane if that's what it's going to take to be at peace with her God. Again and again, she demonstrates a readiness to learn, to understand, and question. And over and over again, she is shown something far greater and more mysterious than anything she can muster, bigger and more powerful than the men who dominate her or the culture that subordinates her. It's during these frequent moments of humility that Janie emerges as a force of greatness. Her power as a heroine doesn't beat you over the head; it smolders quietly, unseen and unacknowledged by all except the forces that count in the end.

A modern heroine's trials may seem more internal than sweeping, but each one is an opportunity to prove her own mettle. The destination, the vehicle, are beside the point: faith can be expressed in one's self as well as in any church. It's all in the balance between inner conviction and external storm. Even the most faithful among us have their occasional crises, whether brought on by spiritual malaise or moral quandary. And Zora Neale Hurston has given us something to take with us on the way: a document of her own conviction, struggle and doubt, a heroine who questions and fights right alongside us, staring down the hurricane that exposes both her frailty and her faithfulness.

I know I'm not the only person who finishes *Their Eyes Were Watching God* with a sigh of mixed relief and longing. It can be intimidating to walk into faith with a woman who pursued it in its most extreme and forceful expressions and who articulated hers so fearlessly. It's certainly exhausting to place ourselves in the hands of an author for whom work, life, and faith melded and meshed so seamlessly. But Zora is a good guide, offering two alternatives in one heroine who forges through a hurricane even as she questions her purpose on Earth. Zora didn't shy away from the ancient ritual, the pungent fruit, but she hands us our share in manageable bites. In the pages of *Their Eyes Were Watching God*, she's always there to remind us that, even if the storm gets up in our nostrils and tears out all our hair, we're still protected, still capable of moving forward on faith's road.

A keen anthropologist, a wordsmith with a divine mission, Zora admired her culture for daring to "call old gods by a new name." As heroines, we must practice that courage daily as we seek our own truths. The flip side of faith is having faith placed in us by others. Sadly, neither Zora nor Janie really received that honor during their lifetimes. That's something we can rectify as we look for company on our way down faith's path. As I cultivate faith in myself and strive to deserve the trust others place in me, I have two companions at the ready: both Janie Crawford and the truth-stretcher and truth-seeker that cohabited Zora's vibrant soul.

READ THIS BOOK:

- When you're not sure if you're going to church or going through the motions
- At first sight of external or internal hurricanes
- When your cares seem trivial in the face of depressing world events

JANIE'S LITERARY SISTERS:

- Maya Angelou in *I Know Why the Caged Bird Sings*
- Edna Pontellier in *The Awakening*, by Kate Chopin
- Kristin Lavransdatter in *The Wreath*, by Sigrid Undset

CHAPTER 3

HAPPINESS

Anne Shirley in *Anne of Green Gables*, by Lucy Maud Montgomery

> "You see before you a perfectly happy person,
> Marilla," she announced. "I'm perfectly happy—
> yes, in spite of my red hair. Just at present I have
> a soul above red hair."

LUCY MAUD MONTGOMERY, *ANNE OF GREEN GABLES*

The winter of 1905 wasn't exactly what you would call happy; in fact, it was the worst winter in recent memory. Cavendish, Prince Edward Island, had frozen from picturesque small town to somber icicle, its quaint roads and houses shut in by huge drifts of snow. The fitful ocean had long since frozen over in spots, preventing even the hardiest icebreakers from reaching the island with their vital cargoes of food and mail. Trapped inside her grandmother's kitchen,

Lucy Maud Montgomery may have been the snowed-in town's most discontented resident.

Maud had good reason to be unhappy. Her thirtieth birthday had come and gone the year before, leaving her no closer to a settled, independent life. Still unmarried, she depended on her crotchety grandmother, Lucy Woolner Macneill, for shelter. The cabin fever of that winter was just another chapter in a life so far marked by abandonment, loss, and lack of stimulation.

Restless, testy, and depressed, Maud wasn't exactly poised to live up to a heroine's promise. And nobody in frozen Cavendish—not even Maud herself—could have predicted that this troubled woman would create one of the happiest heroines in literature.

She inherited her propensity for great despair, but also great happiness, from the stormy islet itself. Prince Edward Island wasn't always an icy prison: in summer, it was a verdant paradise full of flowers, fields, and landscapes that perfectly suited a moody, almost-orphaned child. Maud didn't lose both parents as a baby like the typical charity case, but she still received an orphan's upbringing. Her mother Clara died of pneumonia when Maud was only two, leaving her to the occasional care of a dashing and neglectful father, Hugh "Monty" Montgomery. Unwilling or unable to take responsibility for his daughter, he left Maud with her maternal grandparents, Alexander and Lucy Woolner Macneill, and set out to make his fortune without the encumbrance of a dreamy young child.

Lonely and confused by her father's wayward life, Maud found it hard to live with her grandparents. The couple was old, strict, irascible—qualities that sometimes threatened to stifle their expressive granddaughter's spirit. Though there was some pleasure in those early years, Maud was never allowed to forget that she was homeless and unloved. She dreamed of joining her father and escaping her stern upbringing forever.

When given the opportunity to rejoin Monty, who had remarried and moved to Prince Albert, Saskatchewan, 2,700 miles away, she jumped at the chance to buck her grandparents' iron rule. The long train ride was full of hopes and dreams. Emotionally starved, she gave her father all of the qualities her current life lacked—sensitivity, flair, and romance. Little did she know her trip would be a journey to nowhere.

Maud arrived in Prince Albert and found her father preoccupied, her stepmother distant. Their expectations immediately clashed. Instead of the welcome she had craved, Maud found a family relieved to have another set of hands.

The realization that she was to be no more than a glorified babysitter—and that her education would gladly be placed on hold so that she could carry out this expected drudgery—was a crushing blow to sensitive Maud. Her family fantasy shattered, she returned home in less than a year. Even the strictures of the Macneill household were infinitely preferable to her father's scattered and conditional love. She returned to her grandparents' home to study, teach school, and wait for life to improve.

Cavendish's newest teacher wasn't just well educated: she had grown into a stylish, even vain young woman. Though her marriage prospects still seemed slender due to her poverty, Maud began to feel the power of flirtation and sophistication. Somehow, despite her strict upbringing and her grandparents' clannish, interior ways, she managed to string together a long chain of beaux, culminating in what she would call "The Year of Mad Passion" ever afterward.

At first it seemed as if 1897 would be the end to Maud's troubles. After all, it was the year in which she discovered the intoxicating power of her own sweet self. First, she attracted the attentions—and the intentions—of a handsome theology student who made a bright impression on her sensitive psyche. Edwin Simpson was flirtatious, daring, and cosmopolitan—everything that oppressively rural Cavendish was not. Their flirtation became a fervent correspondence and finally, at Maud's insistence, a secret engagement. But the mad passion wasn't over yet. Though her heart was busy elsewhere, Maud's body somehow got caught up in a forbidden obsession with Herman Leard, a local farmer whose attentions she simultaneously encouraged and feared.

They met late at night, driven into each other's arms as much by the secrecy of their relationship as its physical intensity. Her desire ignited, Maud dabbled with the idea of indulging it fully. But when Herman finally propositioned her, fear of pregnancy, her engagement to Edwin, and the lessons of a chaste upbringing overrode her body's demands. Was he appealing? Yes. Was he appropriate? No. Maud had promised herself she'd only give herself to a man worthy of his prize. "Impossible," she concluded. She ended both relationships, perhaps thankful that Herman's kisses had highlighted Edwin's shortcomings.

The period that followed the Year of Mad Passion could have easily been dubbed "The Years of Intense Frustration." Self-sacrifice seemed like the only option for Maud, alone for now. She grudgingly quit teaching and moved in with her grandmother upon her grandfather's death, though he pointedly left Maud out of his will. Then the tragedies started: Herman died unexpectedly in 1899, and Maud had to close the door on her desire for good. And any fantasies she still harbored about her father died with him in 1900. To make matters worse, Grandmother Macneill was a testy living companion, whether due to dementia or just cranky old age. The increasing gap between Maud's inner life and outer reality wasn't just striking, it was depressing.

Annoyed and dejected, Maud threw herself into reading and writing, a pastime she had taken up secretively since graduating from college. The farmhouse's tiny kitchen served as the community's post office, giving Maud the perfect means by which to secretly submit and track the progress of the stories she had begun to send to magazines and newspapers around North America. But even that pleasure faded in the winter of 1905. Isolated from the mainland and in the grips of a brutal winter storm, Maud felt trapped and miserable.

It was during those long winter months that Maud relived her greatest unhappiness: the solitary childhood that had created a sensitive, imaginative, and painfully lonely woman. Housebound, Maud reached something near despair during those lonesome months. Cut off from reality, left with only her old journal entries and letters to reread, she became more and more depressed.

Amazingly, the first seeds of spring were sown with those recollections. For by the time the buds returned to the trees, Maud's own imagination and pen had thawed. The seed she planted was a girl, almost inseparable from the girl Maud had been years ago. And the fruit it bore has long outlived its creator.

To understand the heroine of *Anne of Green Gables*, you must first know what she isn't. Anne Shirley is not a boy. And that's where all the trouble begins.

When Matthew and Marilla Cuthbert, a brother and sister set in their ways and their simple country existence, send off for an orphan to help around the farm, they have no idea they're going to receive a redheaded, motormouthed, imaginative, and utterly unorthodox girl instead of the obedient boy they ordered. But arrive she does, cracking open the Cuthberts' quiet lives along the way.

As she makes her way in Avonlea, a rural town that gives Cavendish a run for its money in terms of lack of imagination, Anne gets herself into an endless series of scrapes and mishaps. She inspires the teasing and then the competition of Gilbert Blythe, the handsome young boy who loses her respect after he makes fun of her red hair. She infuriates Mrs. Rachel Lynde, the town's resident busybody, with her lack of manners. And—awkwardly, miserably, slowly—she becomes a young woman and a community pillar, transforming herself from outcast orphan to everyone's child.

For a girl with a start in misery, Anne Shirley sure doesn't realize it. True, she's lonely, lowly, and doomed to perpetual ridicule for her one distinctive feature—her bright red hair. But unlike her creator, she's skilled at making the best and brightest of every situation. It's certainly not what you'd think would come from the pen of a woman who felt so stifled and out of place in her own home. Anne, unlike Maud, has a capacity to create happiness where she sees none. Her overactive imagination immediately goes to work in even the most distasteful situation, transforming a nasty pond into a Lake of Shining Waters and a tree in bloom into a beautiful bride.

Even despair can be delicious to such an imaginative heroine. Anne's all-or-nothing approach extends to her miseries, which are as overblown and intense as her author's. Consider her ecstasy of sadness when she whips herself into an emotional frenzy over the imagined wedding of Diana Barry, her best friend:

"Whatever's the matter now, Anne?" [Marilla] asked.

"It's about Diana," sobbed Anne luxuriously. "I love Diana so, Marilla. I cannot ever live without her.

But I know very well when we grow up that Diana will get married and go away and leave me. And oh, what shall I do? I hate her husband—I just hate him furiously. I've been imagining it all out—the wedding and everything—Diana dressed in snowy garments, with a veil, and looking as beautiful and regal as a queen; and me the bridesmaid, with a lovely dress, too, and puffed sleeves, but with a breaking heart hid beneath my smiling face. And then bidding Diana goodbye-e-e—" Here Anne broke down entirely and wept with increasing bitterness.

Here is a happy heroine: a girl contented to talk to her reflection in a mirror, who does her best to imagine puffed sleeves on plain calico dresses. Here is a heroine who glides through Avonlea's fields, gardens, and meadows in blissful reverie, who breaks her slate over Gilbert Blythe's head in vain anger and hurt feelings. She dares to walk the ridgepole of Mr. Barry's kitchen roof with a casual bravado that anxious Maud, who could not abide even a drawbridge, could never hope to replicate.

Like Anne, Maud walked her own fine line. For Maud, the balancing act was between her desolate nature and her highest hopes. Some of these she expressed in her books:

the ways in which Anne inverts Maud's own struggles are as poignant as the ways in which she reflects them. Given a lonely, abusive childhood (Anne is shuffled off from home to home and treated as less than a servant before arriving at Green Gables), Anne manages to find happiness in the unlikeliest places. Though she shares parts of Maud's personality—touchy vanity, passionate hopes, runaway dreams—Anne has far fewer boundaries and hang-ups than her creator. Scared and scarred, Maud withheld affection for others and hid her true thoughts from one and all; in contrast, Anne approaches life with trust and unconditional love.

Take Anne's unconventional arrival at Green Gables. Blissfully unaware that she'll be shipped back to the orphanage the next day, Anne introduces herself to Matthew Cuthbert and readers in a rapturous monologue that is happiness itself. The next morning, she befriends the tree outside her window and awaits her fate. But her happiest moment is the one in which she's told that she belongs:

"I'm crying," said Anne in a tone of bewilderment. "I can't think why. I'm glad as glad can be. Oh, GLAD doesn't seem the right word at all. I was glad about the White Way and the cherry blossoms—but this! Oh, it's something more than glad. I'm so happy. I'll try to be so good. It will be uphill work, I expect, for Mrs. Thomas often told me I was desperately wicked. However, I'll do my very best. But can you tell me why I'm crying?"

Though she had trouble enacting it in her everyday life, Maud passionately believed that creativity could transform the negative into something positive. She wrote this into her spunky heroine, creating a girl who translates her lonely childhood into a useful young womanhood. When Diana's sister comes down with the croup, estranged Anne takes the experience of her neglected, overburdened childhood and turns it into something wonderful. Ipecac-soaked and full of hacking coughs, Minnie Mae's rescue is more than just a close escape. It's redemption, Maud-style . . . sadness translated into joy à la Anne Shirley. And it's even more powerful when we learn that Maud herself unsuccessfully nursed her young cousin Katie, who died of pneumonia on her watch in 1904.

No, Anne isn't content to merely transform trees into buddies and sinking boats into romantic biers. Her mission is greater and harder: armed with an extravagant imagination and a loud mouth, she sets out to change an entire town's worldview—and succeeds.

Any woman who grew up thinking Marilla was bitchy and unapproachable should run, not walk, to the bookshelf and reread *Anne*. Over the course of the book, we see a familiar old spinster encounter a force of nature—and learn to love it. Just as Anne shatters the provincial town's preconceptions of what to expect from an anonymous orphan girl with devilish red hair, she also explodes plain Marilla's idea of what it's like to love and be loved. We need only to watch Marilla secretly snuggle with a sleeping Anne to realize that a true transformation has occurred.

But for all of Anne's happiness, there's a bittersweetness to the *Anne* books that can be traced directly back to their creator. 1905, the year that birthed Anne, was the start of Maud's own tentative attempt to balance happiness and despair. During the turbulent year in which she penned her first successful novel, Maud was not just immersed in the story of her "red-headed snippet"; she was faced with the most important choice of her life. Vain Maud loved to flirt and knew she would not easily be wooed; comfortable with subterfuge and mystery, she tried to keep her newest admirer, attractive Presbyterian minister Ewan Macdonald, at a comfortable distance.

But as her book neared completion, Maud's own walls fell. She succumbed to Ewan's measured courtship despite serious concerns about his temperament and prospects. *Anne of Green Gables* was already finished and making the rounds with publishers when Maud made her final decision, opting for the security of a home and a stable income in spite of her questions about Ewan's stringent Presbyterianism and her concerns about the even stricter role of a minister's wife. When *Anne of Green Gables* was published in 1908, Maud's engagement was still a secret. She married Ewan only after the death of her grandmother in 1911.

Maud paid a heavy price for her supposed happiness; married life was not what she had bargained for. Unable or unwilling to purchase her own home through the proceeds of what was by now one of the most successful children's books of its time, Maud opted instead to let Ewan make all the decisions. She followed him away from the island, experiencing increasing homesickness, isolation, and grief at their new home in Ontario. The years that followed would bring a child's death, the onset of a devastating world war, and an exhausting legal battle with Maud's publishers. Worse still was the loneliness Maud suffered every day. Ewan had waffled between attentive and distant during their six-year courtship, but once they married, things changed. He turned out to be mentally ill, abandoning her during his many nervous breakdowns.

Throughout her long marriage, self-censoring Maud was often silent on her loneliness, despair, and depression. She was accompanied by her happy heroine for the rest of her life, penning nine sequels and gaining international literary acclaim. But eventually Maud herself gave up the balancing act, exhausted by a tightrope walk that had stolen over thirty years of her life. In 2008, her family revealed that her 1942 death, formerly thought to be of congestive heart failure, was actually due to a self-inflicted drug overdose.

What is there for a modern heroine to learn from Maud's own sad story? Surely a woman who went to such lengths to conceal her inner struggles, carefully commenting on her diaries and destroying inconvenient letters, doesn't have much to teach about happiness. But Maud left us Anne, and Anne's passionate embrace of now. That contradiction, and Anne's own story of books not quite matching their covers, is a powerful reminder that internal and external circumstances don't always match. Even if Maud wasn't capable of living out true happiness, she gave it to generations of girls and women all over the world through books that have long outlasted her unhappy life. The most pleasant and vivacious person among us still has inner battles to fight; the ugliest orphan can bring beauty and love to her new world.

As modern heroines, we may have been teased for the color of our hair, but hopefully none of us has ever been told that our not-boyness is an unacceptable disappointment. No matter: Anne's story belongs to us even if we've never laid eyes on a bottle of raspberry cordial. So what if Anne's desperate longing to fit in is manifested in a passionate but outdated interest in puffed sleeves and the grandness of spare bedrooms? It doesn't mean her story is any less powerful or relevant today.

As a weird, melodramatic child, I longed to do or say the one thing that would make me just like all other girls, no matter what the cost. It's the kind of impulse that leads a girl to douse herself in Love's Baby Soft or cover herself in hideous-but-stylish early 1990s flannels that threaten to engulf her entire teenage frame. This need to fit in at all costs smacks of reality-show antics designed to attract Z-list fame. It's the enemy of progress and of self-esteem, something that drives a heroine off her higher path and into a world of trivialities and bad decisions. Yes, it's hard to be a Cate Blanchett when you feel like a desperate Heidi

Montag inside, but it's not too hard to choose between the two.

Anne succumbs to that impulse, too. Tempted by what others possess, she accidentally dyes her red hair green, and gets Diana drunk on currant wine she mistakes for raspberry cordial in a dreadful parody of a proper visit. Every time she fumbles, she is reminded that happiness lies within, not in the trappings of a rich or popular girl. She isn't a heroine because she finally gets the puffed sleeves she covets; she's memorable for the little things, the spring-time walks through verdant fields, her insistence on playing Tennyson's Elaine in a sinking dinghy, the strength of her passionate likes and dislikes.

Elegant adult Anne will never leave gawky, self-hating Anne-who'd-rather-be-called-Cordelia altogether behind, but as the book progresses she focuses far more on what she has than on what she thinks she wants. Once she learns to trust that inner source of happiness, she's free to be the Anne everyone loves—dreamy, impractical, fresh, and eternally unique. It's not surprising that this Anne, who boldly flavors cake with anodyne liniment and tells off the town busybody, reflects the most appealing qualities of her creator. But Anne's embrace of her own self, her fear-less pursuit of her own happiness, is as much a cautionary tale as an inspirational one. Like the girl who falls off the kitchen roof and breaks her ankle due to her fear of unpopularity, a heroine is better served when she opts for internal pleasure rather than appeasing others. And like Anne, we'd do well to cultivate happiness on the inside in the hopes that we'll start to see it all around. Yes, there is something to be said for happiness. Just ask Maud:

"One of the reviews says 'the book radiates happiness and optimism,' " she wrote in her journal in 1908, shortly after the publication of *Anne of Green Gables*. "When I think of the conditions of worry and gloom and care under which it was written I wonder at this. Thank God, I can keep the shadows of my life out of my work. I would not wish to darken any other life—I want instead to be a messenger of optimism and sunshine."

READ THIS BOOK:

- When someone repeatedly misspells your name or implies that they'd rather interact with a man
- When life gives you wrinkled yoga pants instead of puffed sleeves
- At three in the morning when you can't stop coughing and are propped up in bed, drowsy and discontented

ANNE'S LITERARY SISTERS:

- Betsy Ray in Maud Hart Lovelace's Betsy-Tacy series
- Ramona in *Beezus and Ramona*, by Beverly Cleary
- Flora Poste in *Cold Comfort Farm*, by Stella Gibbons

CHAPTER 4

DIGNITY

Celie in *The Color Purple*, by Alice Walker

> The most common way people give up their power
> is by thinking they don't have any.
>
> **ALICE WALKER**

What's a heroine to do when her very existence is threatened and denied? If she's anything like Alice Walker, she fights back. That Alice, the future author of *The Color Purple*, could transcend her own challenging beginnings wasn't immediately evident when she came into the world in 1944. The youngest of eight children, Alice was the daughter of cash-strapped sharecroppers trying to eke out a living in rural Georgia against astonishing odds.

Sharecropping, that oppressive system of rock-bottom wages and backbreaking labor, was still alive and well in the rural South, where working black families earned a fraction of the salaries made by even unskilled whites. So, too, was Jim Crow segregation. Alice's childhood world was one where blacks and whites could not dine in the same restaurant. Her family had to enter the movie theater from a separate entrance and sit far overhead in the sweaty, stifling balcony. And she had to witness the indignities that her fellow blacks suffered on an unremitting basis.

The Walkers had barely survived the Great Depression. Her father Willie Lee worked the fields, sometimes barely scraping up $300 in one year. Often, his year's work would be completely canceled out by the unfairly inflated prices of rent and dry goods that the property owner insisted on. To make ends meet, Alice's mother Minnie went out as a maid and worked in the fields herself, her labors interrupted but not halted by the long succession of children she bore. When Alice, the baby, was born, Minnie was unable to take any kind of leave. As soon as she could stand again, she was back in the fields.

Indignity, poverty, and hard times didn't affect Minnie's unshakable sense of self . . . or Willie's insistence on strict gender roles. While the sons of the family were encouraged to sow their wild oats, the girls were constantly watched and subjected to a higher standard of conduct. Blacks, too, were expected to comport themselves so well that they were unassailable, an impossible task in a culture so imbued with white good, black bad sentiment. Still, stubborn Minnie refused to bow down to the whites in Eatonton, Georgia. When she was verbally abused by a woman who thought she was too well dressed to receive relief, Minnie stood her ground and insisted on receiving the flour that was her due. She was kicked out of the aid office, but the incident was characteristic of Minnie's innate sense of justice and her insistence on humane treatment.

Alice read and wrote early, excelling in school and showing every sign of promise by 1952. But tragedy struck that year. During a rambunctious game of Cowboys and Indians, the eight-year-old was shot in the eye with a BB by one of her brothers. Ashamed and scared of the repercussions, the boys initially insisted she lie about the wound and say it was no big deal. By the time her parents realized it was severe, they could not find a car with which to transport her to the nearest doctor. They nursed Alice at home, springing for treatment only after her father borrowed $250, an astronomical sum for the family, from his boss to pay for a doctor's visit. The prejudiced doctor prescribed some eye drops, pocketed the money, and sent Alice home to "heal." Her recovery was agonizing and dangerous. By the time the pain subsided, she was completely blind in her right eye. Worse than partial blindness was the huge cataract that remained, an ugly reminder she saw every time she looked in the mirror.

Alice's appearance wasn't all that changed. Her personality, once sassy and bright, became subdued and internal. She was made fun of at school and even lived with her grandparents temporarily to escape the ridicule of her classmates. Bewildered and hurt, she resented that her brothers had not been punished in any way for their part in what she saw as a hideous disfigurement. Her brothers' betrayal was made even more intense by the gag rule her family seemed to have imposed on any talk about Alice's injury. She was left to feel out her way in silence. It's no wonder that books, poetry, and writing became her solace during this time.

In 1958, her older brother intervened. Bill, who had moved with his wife to Boston to seek better work, invited fourteen-year-old Alice to visit him and took her to a doctor who removed the unsightly cataract. Her self-confidence restored along with her eyesight, Alice returned home and went on to excel in school. She rose to academic and social success, graduating as the school valedictorian with a scholarship to prim Spelman College in 1961. But though Alice met her influential mentor, Howard Zinn, at Spelman and became engaged in the civil rights movement, it was ultimately too prissy, polite, and constrained for her liking. She transferred to Sarah Lawrence in New York, beginning her tutelage in feminist ideologies and social activism in earnest.

During the 1960s, it seemed as if the entire country was learning how to work together toward social ends. As the chaotic, sometimes violent forces of the civil rights movement, second-wave feminism, and protest against the war in Vietnam converged, Alice found herself surrounded by radical thinkers, people who taught her that change had to start at home. When she graduated, she took a position as a welfare administrator. Alice Walker was ready to practice what she preached.

When the opportunity to work for the NAACP's Defense Legal Fund in Mississippi presented itself, she jumped at the chance. Mississippi was a hotbed for racial discrimination and Jim Crow. It was the last place she expected to meet and fall in love with a white Jewish lawyer named Mel Leventhal. They married in New York in 1967 and immediately took a risky chance, moving to Jackson, Mississippi, as civil rights workers. Interracial marriage wasn't just unrecognized in Mississippi; it was illegal. Alice's family was shocked, both by their independent daughter's choice to marry and by the young couple's audacity. Mel's mother responded by cutting her son out of her life entirely. But the young couple, passionately involved in their work, shook off threats, doubts, and physical intimidation and moved to Jackson anyway. It would take more than a few bullies to beat them.

During her time doing civil rights work in Mississippi, Alice learned the true extent of Jim Crow's decimation of black dignity, especially that of females who had almost no legal protection and who were disregarded and marginalized. In a time when demanding a seat on the bus for a pregnant black woman was still a political act, Alice Walker herself was pregnant and engaged in what would become her most important political work: writing, and writing well. Her blinded eye had given her a new lens on human suffering when she was a child. Armed with what she had seen in Mississippi and secure in her survivor status, she was ready to turn that eye on the suffering of others.

Alice's daughter, Rebecca Grant Leventhal, was a beautiful baby. For Alice, she symbolized the kind of potential the new mother envisioned for a country in turmoil. But life with a small child of mixed race was not easy in prejudiced Mississippi. Alice began to tire of the constant threats, the unwanted attention when walking down the street, the hostility she and her husband had to endure on a daily basis. She herself was criticized within the civil rights movement as a race traitor who had sold herself in marriage to the oppressor. And Jackson's intellectual life was less than stimulating.

Though politics and protest were in her blood, Alice's experiences in Mississippi were stifling her craft. When she was offered a writing fellowship at Radcliffe College in Cambridge, Massachusetts, she was faced with a difficult decision. Should she stay with her husband in a city that was strangling her creative life, or pursue her passion for writing in an intellectual community that could feed her greater potential? After some soul-searching, the decision was final. She moved to Massachusetts with Rebecca, leaving her marriage on hold and Mississippi far behind. Though she initially hoped to keep her relationship with her husband alive, it stagnated and failed. The couple divorced in 1967, leaving Alice free to follow her literary passion throughout one of the most fruitful periods of her life.

Even as she produced her own groundbreaking work, Alice was quick to acknowledge the legacy of the trailblazers who had come before her. She fought to revive the legacy of Zora Neale Hurston, whose work had been all but forgotten following false accusations of child molestation.

She taught a groundbreaking course at Wellesley on the black woman writer, a class whose reverberations would be felt through an entire generation of authors. And she championed members of the growing "Sisterhood" group of women writers, like Toni Morrison and June Jordan.

It is this sense of legacy, history, and cultural rootedness that we tap into the moment we crack open *The Color Purple*, Alice's most beloved work and the winner of the 1983 Pulitzer Prize in Fiction. But more than history and sisterhood, *The Color Purple* is a book about dignity: dignity threatened, taken away; dignity unearthed and redeemed. The story is told through the letters of Celie, a poor black woman whose life has been a series of injustices. Raped, beaten, and forced to marry a man she does not love, Celie has no dignity at all. Even worse than her physical domination is what has happened to her mind: she has internalized the abuse heaped upon her and all women in her company, mirroring her brutal husband's distrust of the strong Sofia and her husband's mistress, Shug Avery.

Throughout the book, women forge uneasy bonds that mirror those Alice Walker created during her life. Even as unlikely couples come together and drift apart, one woman manages to reclaim her own dignity. First she finds it in her body, in a same-sex love affair that shocks her as much as it awakens her. Then she finds it in commerce and finally in family ties. *The Color Purple* is a story of concentric circles, but at the center of that tenuous Venn diagram is one thing: Celie's worth as a woman and a human.

Again and again, Alice points toward women's bonds as transformative and dignified, especially in a time that frowns upon same-sex relationships and family claims. One of the most heartbreaking offenses of Mr. _____ is his denial of Celie's family ties, a denial that negates the very thing that keeps her human in the face of such inhumanity. By cutting Celie off from her family, Mr. _____ plays out the role of the perfect abuser, someone who exerts control for the sake of his ego, who would take away someone else's soul before he'd let go of her body. Throughout these passages, Alice seems to point to the fact that women must seek one another for companionship and solace, whether or not they look to one another for sexual pleasure. Cleaving to the relationships that make us whole is a way of claiming power and retaining self-esteem.

The true disenfranchisement Alice portrays in her book is shocking, but it is representative of the reality of thousands of black women who were subject to abuse, humiliation, and daily deprivation in a society that respected neither their race nor their gender. In *The Color Purple*, we can see

Alice reaching back toward her mother and grandmother, both raised in slavelike conditions in the segregated South, and the generations of slaves who came before them. Her narrative spans continents and generations, but at its heart is always that burning question of a woman's worth.

Where is Celie's dignity? It has been taken away from her by the men who rape her, the culture that insists she is worthless, her illiteracy, and the economic insecurity that assures she will never transcend the place in which she was born. But just as her dignity is there for the taking by those who would abuse her, it is there for her own discovery. *The Color Purple* is no Cinderella story, but its happy ending relies on Celie's sense of self-esteem being right where it should be: inside herself, and belonging to her alone.

Bolstered in part by Alice's insistence on dignity and in part by writing that explodes and reinvents the epistolary novel, *The Color Purple* emerged to much fanfare in 1982. But mixed in with the praise, the attention, and the rewards were serious criticisms. The book was challenged and banned repeatedly, derided for its "uneducated" speech, criticized for its exposure of abuse and inequality within the black community. Luckily, Alice Walker's book of salvation was a huge commercial success despite its many denouncers, resulting in a critically acclaimed movie directed by Steven Spielberg and starring Oprah Winfrey and Whoopi Goldberg.

For Walker herself, salvation has been a rough road to tread. Success carried a heavy price, from the constant attacks on *The Color Purple* and her subsequent works to strife with family members who couldn't fully embrace her new fame. Rebecca resented what she saw as Alice's absenteeism; Alice's longtime lover, Robert Allen, blamed his repeated affairs on Alice's thriving career. Meanwhile, Alice dabbled with her love for women, blending the philosophical and personal as she publicly embraced her bisexuality.

Alice has stuck to her radical politics, remaining active in the antiwar, civil rights, and feminist movements. Her checkered personal life, particularly her very public estrangement from her daughter, has been a rocky sticking point for fans and critics alike. But Alice is a woman who knows how to withstand and weather the criticisms and misgivings of others, even in the cruel arena of literary superstardom. Just as she re-created a literary form in *The Color Purple*, she has redefined herself multiple times, embracing and then toppling terms like bisexual, vegan, and feminist. Alice remains an activist and a warrior, fighting for awareness of political issues like voter registration, female genital mutilation, and the cause of political prisoner

Mumia Abu-Jamal. And she continues to write, solidifying her position as one of the most prolific and poignant voices of our time.

It's easy to read about a time and mindset I'll never experience firsthand, but it's harder to write about it with any sense of authority. Who am I, a white woman in a world that's relatively kind to white women, to stare down a work of fiction that contains injustices I'm privileged enough never to have to worry about? Luckily, Alice makes it easy to enter that world through her complex heroine. Not everyone will be beaten and taunted by the man they're forced to marry; not everyone will be so isolated that their only outlet is to write letters to God. Hell, we live in a world with an African-American president and an increasingly diverse selection of heroines of color. That may be as it should, but it's not a panacea. That's why we need books like *The Color Purple*. It's tempting to dismiss Celie's story as extreme, but to do so would be to miss the point entirely. The very universality of her struggle is what makes it so terrifying. Celie could be any number of black women in the South of just a few years ago. And her fumbling journey toward self-love is so universal that she could be any one of us, too.

For me, *The Color Purple* is like a big loud flag being

waved in the face of complacency, ruffling up the part of me that would rather turn away from ugliness and brutality. Alice is the one waving that flag, shoving me, nicking away at my prejudices and privilege with her pen. Celie is a bit gentler, but don't mistake the simple survival instinct of her actions for stupidity or irrelevance. Faced as she is with an intolerable life and a cruel relationship dynamic, every one of Celie's simplest actions is imbued with worth and weight. In Celie's world, getting up in the morning is an astonishing claim to dignity, let alone falling in love with another woman or daring to read the letters that Mr. _____ has tried to hide from her. Each act of life, no matter how small, reaffirms Celie's worth and self-respect. It makes me wonder how many times my simple acts have served a greater purpose. Perhaps my smallest decisions are some kind of foundation, a cornerstone for who I am as a person and who I am entitled to be.

Alice Walker has never been one to do small. When she saw injustice in the place she was born, she went back, intent on rectifying it. When she sees dignity threatened and trodden upon all around her, you're safe to bet that she'll fight it with all the force of her pen. Are heroines obligated to stage impressive feats in the fight for dignity, or can we act in smaller ways? Surely Alice and Celie's real and fictitious life experiences point to different, equally valid approaches. Both warn against complacency, the enemy of action and of dignity. When we turn our eyes away from anything, be it injustice or the color purple, our heroine's value is debased and denied. When we look life in the face, we may shy away from what we see. In Alice Walker's world and in ours, there are too many things designed to knock a heroine's teeth out, keeping her silent and small. But if Alice and Celie are to be our guides, we must learn that to give in to the threat is to give it all of our power. When we shy away from the task, we strangle ourselves. When we face it with all the force of our dignity as women and as heroines, things change for the better, however slowly or simply.

We may never develop Alice Walker's own uncompromising vision, the power to keep looking at the fire even when we're half blind. But we can practice, question, and reaffirm ourselves even when we'd rather leave indignity and brutality safely between the covers of a book. There's a time for both the sweeping gesture and the smaller one. There's always time for dignity, even if we can only lay claim to our own in Celie's simple acceptance of what is: "I'm pore, I'm black, I may be ugly and can't cook. . . . But I'm here."

READ THIS BOOK:

- When complacent or a bit too contented
- Before important elections or contentious board meetings
- With your teenage daughters

CELIE'S LITERARY SISTERS:

- Sethe in *Beloved*, by Toni Morrison
- Offred in *The Handmaid's Tale*, by Margaret Atwood
- Idgie Threadgood in *Fried Green Tomatoes at the Whistle Stop Café*, by Fannie Flagg

CHAPTER 5

FAMILY TIES

Francie Nolan in *A Tree Grows in Brooklyn*, by Betty Smith

We never understood each other, Mother. And I know I gave you a hard time. . . . It was because I wanted you to talk to me. I know now why I told you so many lies, Mother. I wanted you to notice me. And I didn't mind it too much when you scolded me.

I would rather have had you scold me, Mother, than ignore me.

BETTY SMITH

My dad grumbled as he grudgingly forked over the $100 overweight fee to an impatient airline attendant. I fidgeted with my carry-on, eager at the age of fifteen to be shipped off to unknown territory along with two bulky suitcases. Headed to an unknown country and armed with only two words in German ("thanks" and "potato"), I only had room for one work of fiction in my bag. I had a suspicion that I'd need something, anything, in English to sustain me over the year ahead, a year in which my expensive monthly call back home would become something to relish, in which I would be plunged into an awkward family dynamic and separated by more distance than had ever stood between me and my already-tortured family ties.

So what was the book that pushed my baggage over the edge? *A Tree Grows in Brooklyn*, by Betty Smith, a book that has helped me weather so many unfamiliar days and family storms that it shocked me to learn it was written by a woman with a highly ambiguous relationship to her own family.

Throughout her life, it seemed as if Betty Smith was doomed to run away from, parse through, and struggle against her family ties. The little we know for sure about her childhood seems sparse: daughter of immigrants, Elizabeth "Lizzie" Wehner grew up in tenement Brooklyn at the turn of the twentieth century, surrounded by harshness and poverty and denied the love that would later become her obsession. Lizzie was drawn to and cut off from her mother, Katie, a hard woman who passed her florid story-telling style, her bitter survival instinct, and her poverty to her daughter. Not much is known about John Wehner, who died when Lizzie was nineteen. Whatever the details, his life and death burned an irreparable hole through Lizzie's heart, a hole she tried to fill with work, professional accomplishments, and the succession of alcoholic men she doted upon to the detriment of her own physical and mental health.

Faced with a painful home life, Lizzie was eager to create her own family. Her parents forced her to leave school and start working at age fourteen, and insecure, resentful Lizzie quickly moved to associate herself with education and upward mobility. Brooklyn's settlement houses were her social center: there, she danced, debated, studied, and met George Smith, a driven young man who wanted to get out of Brooklyn as much as she did. When he moved to Ann Arbor, Michigan, to study law, she followed. But life as a young wife was no easier than it was during the lean years of her childhood. As she recited her vows to George, Lizzie worried that his brutal schedule, his ambition, and their shared poverty would make it hard to enjoy marriage.

Her premonition was right. Five years later, she was no closer to happiness than she had been before. The intervening years had brought two daughters, Nancy and Mary. Now a young mother, Lizzie felt even more pressure to educate herself. She petitioned to attend the local high school, an unusual request for a married woman. But though she worked hard, life constantly interrupted her studies. Worse still, the man she had followed to this far-off place became more distant with each passing year. It seemed that George's burgeoning legal practice and rising political career had no place for a naive, heavily accented wife. But Lizzie had aspirations of her own. She turned a blind eye to George's affairs and focused instead on her new plan: to become a writer.

Soon, the ledger in which she recorded her literary submissions and sales read like a litany of her own family's emotional and financial ups and downs. Lizzie the woman became Betty Smith the writer, fighting her way into college courses against school regulations that banned students without a high school diploma, writing plays that reflected the dreams of the poor and working classes, even winning the prestigious Avery Hopwood Award for dramatic writing in 1930.

But success couldn't keep Betty's family life from spinning quickly out of her control. Family crises prevailed, crowned by the deaths of Betty's stepfather and George's parents. The distant couple finally uprooted their family, moving east to Amherst, Massachusetts, and then to New Haven, Connecticut, in an uneasy and short-lived reconciliation. The stagnation and fear of her marriage were belied by her professional accomplishments: though she had never officially completed high school, Betty's drama prize allowed her to enroll in graduate studies at Yale. And there she met the man who would puncture her family life for good: a man completely unlike her closed-off husband.

Bob Finch was an artist, an alcoholic, and most importantly, a needy man. He entered her life just as George was moving onward and upward. Left in the dust of her husband's ambitions (he eventually went on to serve in the U.S. Senate and practice before the Supreme Court), Betty focused instead on Bob, a man whose desperation and dramatic nature mirrored her own. She separated from George in 1933.

Alone now with her daughters, Betty struggled as a single mother with no money, no time, and no emotional support. She left Yale and returned to New York, renting an apartment from her again-widowed mother in Queens. But the proximity to her stepfather's memory was painful. Though she never gave details, Betty later hinted that he had sexually abused her. Hungry and concerned about her girls, Betty started selling confession stories to pulp magazines for a few cents a word. The income financed a move to her own apartment a few subway stops away from her mother. The girls came along, attending school and shoveling coal into the furnace while their mother wrote and worked as an actress in Manhattan.

Her children, bewildered by their uprooted life, had started skipping school and were often sick. Betty was able to scrape together enough for long summer trips to a beach cottage, but the girls had to stay there alone as she commuted back to odd jobs in the city. They concealed their misery from Betty, just as she hid hers from them. They had no way of knowing that she worried about them every waking moment, every second that her unrelenting scramble for enough money to survive kept her from them. The Great Depression had come, tearing strong families apart and leaving unprecedented poverty in its wake. But for Betty, this tumultuous era was a vehicle for career success. She had always had an affinity for the underdog, the poor man: now she would be paid to write about him. When federal arts jobs got funding, she was first in line at the employment office.

Betty quickly found her way to the job of her dreams, moving to North Carolina to pursue a federal theater project that sought to bring seasoned artistic professionals to the South. Was she following her literary ambitions or attempting to reconstruct the perfect family? Both: Bob Finch came with Betty to North Carolina.

To Betty and her girls, Chapel Hill was like another world, a place far removed from the gritty, ugly streets of New York. Like the tree she would write about a few years later, Betty was quick to take root. She settled into a small apartment with the girls, befriending the community's most beloved citizens and writing plays as quickly as her ramshackle Smith-Corona could type them. But her financial troubles persisted. The $60 a month George sent for the girls was supplemented by the odd story sale or writing award, but it still wasn't always enough for things like clothing and heat. Now that her daughters were in high school, Betty drew upon her own distant relationship with her mother and allowed them significant freedom. In later years she would learn that this sudden change in attitude had confused her daughters, who longed for their mother's approval and love.

But Betty had other worries. Her ties to Bob had flourished along with her writing, and at first the house had been busy with the impassioned collaboration of two lovers. Bob visited often, filling the house with cheer and humor, but his alcoholism and his constant infidelity wore on Betty. In order to cling to the people she loved, she was constantly called upon to let them go. At one point in the late 1930s she had to ship Mary and Nancy back to their father in

Connecticut because she simply didn't have enough money to make ends meet. She herself could subsist on next to nothing, but the girls couldn't. They wanted to lead normal lives. George grumbled about Betty's failure to provide for her daughters; she, too, worried constantly about her inability to keep her family together. Still she persisted in her writing, sending the girls off to their father during the summers and even using money her daughters found on the ground to buy food for the family.

All along, something inside her compelled her to keep on writing. After making sure the girls had the bare essentials, Betty always turned back to the work that had become all-consuming: an autobiographical novel about her childhood. It took a lot to revisit Brooklyn in her mind, to return to that harsh place where families crowded three or even four generations into the same small apartment, a place rampant with disease, crime, and despair. As she started to spin the story of a skinny, dreamy girl and her hardened mother, she didn't realize she had begun to exorcize childhood demons and communicate with her own daughters. The work that had kept Betty separate from her children's lives for so long was now a conduit of sorts. She wrote while the girls were at school, leaving that day's production in a box next to her desk. As soon as they returned home, her daughters would snatch up the typewritten pages and read more about Francie Nolan and her Brooklyn neighborhood. In its way, *A Tree Grows in Brooklyn* was Betty's gift to them, and to herself.

It's not an easy book to describe or even to read. Grim, even desperate in parts, it takes a steady look at what it's like to be a child whose existence depends on an undependable family in an unbearable state of poverty and want. Like Betty, Francie is obsessed with her dangerously incapable father and repulsed by her make-do mother. Betty's many struggles with love and duty smash into one another in the form of Katie Nolan, a mother who ruins her once-beautiful hands and almost murders a man who would harm a daughter whose brother she favors, whose education she sacrifices to family finances, and whose success she painfully doubts. The book's conflict between mother and child is unsettling and wildly sad. It's also unflinching and real for any woman who has crossed the bridge between childhood and the adult world.

There are many heroines to be had in Francie's Brooklyn, for again and again it is women who form an almost impenetrable circle of support and competence around the lives of their children and husbands. Betty writes her heroines as enemies and saviors at once; her women go through the motions even when the men in their lives are hurt, sick, tired, and incapacitated by drink. They starve for their children's sakes, making a pathetic game out of poverty and starvation, whispering their secrets to one another in the few stolen moments of leisure they somehow manage to wring out of their lives. For Smith, a mother's role is more than that of protector. She's the creator and the destroyer of an entire world.

A Tree Grows in Brooklyn's family ties are about inheritance, the ways in which people obtain weaknesses and peculiarities and beauty just by being born. Tied to each other by bonds they can't explain or even see, Francie's family is as much the head on the table, devastated by the weight of grief, as it is the brother and sister sticking together beneath a brutal neighborhood tradition and a crushing Christmas tree. As Francie loves and hates and fights for self-definition, she often finds that her family is all that stands between her and starvation, abuse, and death.

Luckily for us, Betty Smith doesn't just do blood relations. No, she also gives Francie a chosen family in addition to the one she's born into, a group of kids who clog up Brooklyn's porches and stoops, girls who prepare themselves for their lovers, and shopkeepers whose harassment is as much a part of childhood as Santa Claus. Extended and nontraditional families are just as important as the ones Betty's characters are bonded to genetically. The gentle, golden-hearted aunt whose actions threaten the social order but whose arms are full of love joins a standoffish librarian and gossiping factory workers as people who affect Francie just as much as Johnny Nolan's sidewise singing or Katie's rough-handed attempt at motherly affection. And as she learns to love books, Francie does what we do: assembles an even wider family of fictional characters, using books to help her escape and survive her own family life.

For Betty and Francie, there's nothing clean or simple about family ties. But their very messiness is what makes them so real. When Katie kicks out her sister Sissy for humiliating the family, we can't wait for her to soften and take Sissy back into the fold. The forces that cause a family to stray and fall apart are just as compelling as the ones that glue it back together again.

No matter how terrible the circumstances or crushing the poverty she must endure, Francie sticks to her family identity. It is, after all, the thing that brought her life. It's the thing that keeps her going even when her mother must pretend they are on a polar expedition to help them get through days without any food. It's the thing to which she clings when her teacher tells her to burn the stories she has penned about her father's alcoholism and the "sordid" neighborhood in which she lives:

> Francie went to the big dictionary and looked up the word. Sordid. *Filthy.* Filthy? She thought of her father wearing a fresh dicky and collar every day of his life and shining his worn shoes as often as twice a day. . . . *Also mean and low.* She remembered a hundred and one little tendernesses and acts of thoughtfulness on the part of her father. She remembered how everyone had loved him so. Her face got hot. She couldn't see the next words because the page turned red under her eyes. She turned on Miss Garnder, her face twisted with fury.
>
> "Don't you ever use that word about us!"

When Francie burns the flowery essays she composed to please her teacher, the fantasies she has spun instead of facing the truth about her family, she is doing more than heating up the apartment: she's exorcising herself of other people's opinions of her family. It's a declaration of her family's worth and importance, even in a world that has no use for single mothers or drunken fathers. Francie pays the price in the short term—she falls out of favor with her teacher and loses the academic credit that has meant so much to her—but it's a sacrifice she's more than willing to make for the Nolan family name, even if nobody ever finds out.

Throughout it all, Francie bears witness to a family life that's scarred with tragedy and veined through with fun. Favoritism, alcoholism, and endless poverty threaten to destroy the family unit, but in the end, they only manage to capsize Francie's childhood. Like it or not, Francie is a Nolan, and it's not for nothing that Betty constantly points out the ways in which her heroine combines the hardness of her mother and the weakness of her father, the steeliness of the Rommely women and the dreaminess of the Nolans. A peek into Francie's family hurts and obligations seems to reveal Betty, confused and rebellious about her own unbreakable affinities, working out the tangled skein of her own lineage on the page.

It is exactly these inheritances that challenge a heroine tasked with understanding her family's particular dynamic and creating her own. When Francie fights with her mother about going back to school, you can feel her anxiety about breaking up her already endangered family crawl down your own neck, a spiderlike specter that is guilt, fear, and boldness all tied up in one:

"Our family used to be like a strong cup," thought Francie. "It was whole and sound and held things well. When Papa died, the first crack came. And this fight tonight made another crack. Soon there will be so many cracks that the cup will break and we'll all be pieces instead of a whole thing together. I don't want this to happen, yet I'm deliberately making a deep crack." Her sharp sigh was just like Katie's.

As women charged with creating our own families even as we leave the ones into which we were born, it can feel so wrong to instigate those cracks in the foundation of what we've learned to love. But even as she acknowledges the destructive power of adolescence and adulthood, Betty looks on those rifts with the kindness her mother lacked. Her words are painful, but the underlying message of unity despite the imperfections can help a heroine move through her own disruptions to the family unit.

Betty Smith offers complex solace to heroines called upon to negotiate their own treacherous family roads. In Betty's world, the very man who heals you can be the one who breaks you in two and who sets your life up for a world of pain. The woman who forces you into a life you're not sure you really want is also the person who cares for you most in the world. It's a painful symmetry, one in which the message isn't in the hurting, but in the cleaving to one another.

Francie and Betty both stick to their quest for an intact family. Some abandon their families altogether in favor of an assembled group of friends and fosters. Others, like me, take a clumsy stab at negotiating that gray area that falls between family and self, a mother's love and disapproval, and a daughter's struggle to define her own way. It took much more than my year abroad to teach me that I can allow myself to be part of my family on my own terms, terms we come to in a constant truce of sorts. Decades later, it's slowly sinking in that nobody but me can define what I can contribute to my family, and that my challenge to reconcile myself to my people will be the work of a lifetime, not a day.

As modern heroines, we're faced with an ever-changing definition of *family*. As things like same-sex marriage and changing female roles redefine the family unit, we are called upon to redefine ourselves as heroines and as humans, reassessing and rediscovering our place in relation to others. Whether we're ready to take on the family roles that have been handed us is beside the point. A heroine can create her own familial destiny. Like Francie, we're surrounded by a sloppy, vital, flawed, and abundant family of choice wherever we go. The shining world of childhood might look a bit dingier in the light of day, the librarian may never look up from her desk, even our mothers might falter and fail us on occasion. But as heroines, we can become our own mothers even as we become others'. We can, like Betty Smith, press our backs up against the chimney in our freezing apartment, smuggling the heat of a neighbor's stove as we work on connecting our pasts with our presents.

READ THIS BOOK:

- When you have to make do with $5 until your next paycheck
- After unsettling phone calls with mothers or wild siblings
- On long solo vacations taken to figure out where things stand

FRANCIE'S LITERARY SISTERS:

- Esperanza Cordero in *The House on Mango Street*, by Sandra Cisneros
- Sarah Smolinsky in *The Bread Givers*, by Anzia Yezierska
- Astrid Magnusson in *White Oleander*, by Janet Fitch

CHAPTER 6

INDULGENCE

Claudine in Colette's Claudine novels

I believe there are more urgent and honorable
occupations than the incomparable waste of time
we call suffering.

COLETTE

Paris in the 1890s was a hub of excess, a steaming hothouse
where anything could happen. It was a society that fed on
scandal, cultivated ugliness, stringing together love affairs and louche acts like so many pearls. It was the last
place you'd expect to find Sidonie-Gabrielle Colette, but
there she was, a child among adults, bored and petulant,
barely older than a schoolgirl and still sporting a schoolgirl's knee-length braids. Not exactly a heroine you'd pay
any attention to once you met her husband, Willy, a man
who defined charisma in a charismatic time.

Gabri, as the young wife was known, had a frank provincial accent that stuck in the ears of her new Parisian consorts like burrs in silk. She seemed—and felt—more suited for climbing trees or hiking through the woods than lounging in the stultified, corseted atmosphere of the sitting rooms Willy loved to take her to. A rake, a lecher, a womanizer, and a windbag, Henry "Willy" Gauthier-Villars had an appeal that far outweighed his many weaknesses: Willy was famous, and rabidly so. He had established his reputation as a writer skewering the music of the day and was known for his excessive appetites for food, money, and women. This was a man whose last mistress had committed suicide after bearing his bastard child, a child Willy's parents were eager to dispose of and whom they encouraged Willy to send to sleepy Burgundy to nurse. It's there that he met the Colettes and their seventeen-year-old daughter; before he knew it, he was held captive by her youthful sexuality and her stunning beauty. He would gain nothing by marrying an obscure, dowryless country girl fourteen years his junior, but once he realized that marriage meant he could have her whenever he wanted, he married her all the same.

Gabri herself was more than charmed. She became obsessed with Willy's cravings and the licentious, over-the-top personality that challenged everything her sheltered childhood had taught her. She got to know him a little better during their two-year engagement, but nothing could prepare her for the day in May 1893 when the new wife finally made fin de siècle Paris, in all its tawdry, overdressed glory, her home. Only then did she realize that Willy "specialized" in tomboyish women much younger than himself, women he courted extravagantly and jilted viciously. He enjoyed putting Gabri on display in polite society while he indulged himself in other women's bedrooms. She learned about these affairs first through rumor and anonymous letters, then from chance meetings with her rivals. To a more seasoned woman, one versed in the languid sexuality of bohemian-meets-bourgeois Paris, Willy's flirtations would have seemed harmless. But to Gabri, they were a betrayal.

Caught between a sort of languid love prison and her own growing restlessness, Gabri began to experiment. She didn't dare to take her own lovers (yet), but she could push the envelope in other ways, playing her trophy role to the hilt, daring to wear a boy's sailor suit to social events and reveling in the raised eyebrows and shocked praise of her hosts. She began to collect a shamelessly bohemian group of friends, dramatic and theatrical individuals who challenged social mores. She embraced gay men and demimondaines alike, gathering them around her with her increasingly famous stories of racy schoolgirl life. But even as she tested the boundaries of a stifling social order, her ties to her increasingly money-hungry husband grew stronger. Now she fulfilled the dual role of wife and secretary, handling his correspondence and eventually helping pen his essays.

History does not record whether Gabri (who had begun to tinker with the simple moniker Colette) or Willy first came up with the idea of writing down her schoolgirl stories, but soon enough she was embroiled in a full-scale literary project. It was understood from the start that the work was Willy's. After all, his was the famous name, and he regularly indulged in the very *du jour* practice of employing a stable of ghostwriters whose toil was rewarded by a cut of the royalties—once they agreed to let Willy claim their work as his own. The deal was simple—the writers did the dirty work, Willy took the credit. Why on earth should his arrangement with his wife be any different?

But Willy could have no way of knowing that his young wife was pulling off something quite extraordinary. More impressive than her newfound diligence was the personage her book allowed her to meet, then admire: herself. "I have discovered an astonishing young girl," she told Olympe Terrain in 1896. "Do you know who she is? She's exactly me before my marriage."

"She" is Claudine, the autobiographical heroine of the series that bears her name: a self-portrait of the artist as a restless, sexually frustrated teenager whose extravagance is as boundless as her potential for pleasure. We get the first glimpses of Colette's indulgent future in her first book, *Claudine at School*. Trapped in an inferior school in an obscure provincial French town, Claudine is determined to poke holes in anything and everything, even as she restlessly searches for something to fill up the discomfort that has arisen during her teenage years. There are plenty of distractions while she searches for answers: the drowsy town of Montigny is full of ridiculous, atrociously human characters whose weaknesses Claudine can't resist. School bores and shackles her, but it's not without its charms. There are teachers to lambaste, rules to break, books to mangle, lessons to learn, and students to mock and beat. More appealingly, there are relationships to observe, tease, and secretly long for. Like her little cat Fanchette, Claudine is a sensual creature at heart, flexing and stretching and prowling around in search of someone to scratch her . . . or someone to scratch.

"You're called Claudine, aren't you?"
"Yes. How did you know?"

"Oh, you've been 'talked of' for quite a time. . . . Our mistresses used to say about you: 'She's an intelligent girl but as impudent as a cock-sparrow and her tomboyishness and the way she does her hair set a very bad example' . . . they say you're crazy and more than a bit eccentric."

"Charming women, your teachers! But they're more interested in me than I am in them. So tell them they're only a pack of old maids who are furious because they're running to seed. Tell them that from me, will you?"

Scandalized, she said no more.

Petulant and self-centered, bored and all too aware of her own foolishness, Claudine is a shockingly modern heroine for one who lives in turn-of-the-century France. Constantly on the lookout for diversion and scandal, she creates her own if need be. She compares her breasts to those of her friends, mocking their bodies even as she marvels at her own. She listens hard to adult conversations not fit for childish ears and retaliates against grown-up doubts by acting willfully immature. When forced to look after the younger students at school, she makes them transcribe ridiculous tripe. She refuses to subdue her luxurious hair or behave for the school superintendent, whose licentious looks both thrill and scare her. Disregarding the strict expectations of her era, she leaves school when she pleases, opting instead for long walks through pungent French forests and lazy days at home.

In Claudine's indulgences, we see a bit of the author's own suppressed fervor for life: Claudine *knows* how to act in society, but *chooses* to push boundaries and press buttons at every turn. Hyperaware of her own body, she sets out to see how far she can go, whipping others into an erotic frenzy, then acting the chaste schoolgirl again. And, like any teenager, she realizes that her world is becoming too small to contain her. In a passage that is reminiscent of the coming-of-age chapters in which Francie Nolan realizes that her once-luminous world is cracked and chintzy, Claudine rues her sterile new school and the loss of her childish memories and interests:

Is it because I'm getting older? Can I be feeling the weight of the sixteen years I've nearly attained? That really would be too idiotic for words.

Claudine's indulgence isn't confined to the schoolroom; she falls in love as spectacularly as she flouts convention in school. She doesn't just love, she declares it, after a deliciously drunken night with an older man. She throws herself into marriage and then into sadness, feeling the precariousness of her position as a societal curiosity and a baby bride. And she abandons herself to a passionate love affair with another woman with the blessing of a husband she wishes would object. For Claudine, this outrageous approach to her personal affairs isn't just a means of shocking and gaining attention: it is a declaration of independence in a culture still governed by the corset and the chattel marriage contract, a hypocritical world of appearances and one that gladly overlooks infidelity and abuse as just another side of drawing-room life. It's hard to understand just how torn about city life Colette herself felt until we read about Claudine's struggle to feel at home in her own skin in a controlled, stifling urban setting. And it is possible that Colette didn't understand just how imprisoned she felt before she wrote about it.

Not that the results of her scandalous reminiscences weren't a success. *Claudine at School* was the runaway best seller of 1900. Though Willy initially dismissed the work as childish, yet charming, he reread it and saw a glimmer of his wife's talents . . . and of the pile of money he stood to earn. His name appeared on the cover, and *Claudine* appeared in the drawing rooms of scandalized Paris, whose inhabitants were as intrigued as shocked by the book's frank expressions of sexual longing and disruptive female behavior. How could a book supported by Willy's marketing genius and his wife's teasing, racy voice be anything but a success?

But Colette's triumph was her own prison sentence. The girl who had once longed for sensual domination now found the country house in which Willy sequestered her as a kind of glorified literary slave a bit more than she had bargained for. Worried about money, Willy prodded her to make her next books even more scandalous and titillating. She complied, writing five Claudine novels, two hugely successful plays, and two other books under Willy's name. Isolated and dominated, Colette was a good worker and an assiduous writer. Soon the books became a kind of dialogue in which Colette narrated the ups and downs of her increasingly complicated marriage to Willy, even using her scandalous attachment to a woman named Georgie as fodder for *Claudine Married*. The book was almost banned for its racy content, but not before Colette discovered that Georgie had been bedding Willy, too.

Colette was stunned, both by her lover's unfaithfulness and her husband's. But there wasn't much time to mourn other people's flaws when her own literary daughter had become so unruly. The Claudine novels weren't just popular, they were a phenomenon. Wherever she went, Colette could see mountains of Claudine-branded merchandise . . . and hear whispers about the true authorship of the books. Colette herself was suddenly famous, and she found herself in an increasingly awkward position. Willy now celebrated her androgyny, encouraging her to wear scandalous clothing and insisting on making creepy in-public appearances flanked by his wife and Polaire, a gamine actress who created the Claudine role on the stage. Willy treated them like twin dolls, fondly calling them his "daughters" and, it is to be assumed, bedding them both. Colette played along, but not without a sense of betrayal.

For me, Colette's next move overshadows her more famous future escapades. Sure, she went on to do her time in the theater, where her bare-breasted, passionate kiss with her then-lover, the cross-dressing Mathilde "Missy" de Morny, the marquise of Belboeuf, led to a full-blown art riot. She seduced her sixteen-year-old stepson, engaged in indulgent collaboration with the Vichy regime, even outrageously neglected a daughter who would forever be overshadowed by her famous mother. These moves were all classic Colette, but they could never have happened if it weren't for the stand she took when it came to her first published works. This rebellion started in a social setting, where Colette's frank raconteurism and untutored accent gave away her outsider status. It spilled over into a series of books in which lust and love are turned out at the seams, torn apart, and cobbled back together again in outlandish fashion. And it ended up practiced inside the formerly private confines of a marriage whose shelf life was up and whose inner life she no longer bothered to obscure.

In the end, it wasn't the indiscretions or sleaze that got to Colette. It was the sight of Willy, that infamous dilettante and faux celebrity, co-opting her childhood and her heroine and claiming them as his own. Finally free from the bonds of her first, all-encompassing love and straining under the expectations of a society that neither appreciated nor sustained her, it was time to stake a claim to her most indulgent creation: herself. The details of Colette's battle to get her name on her own literary works could fill their own book. Aware he was being made to look a fool, Willy fought hard for the character he had encouraged and fostered. But the details don't matter much. What counts is that Colette finally fought for her name, gambling on behalf of her heroine and her legendary personal identity.

Must a heroine engage in legal battles, seduce her husband's lover, or mock the very foundations of society in the name of self-indulgence? I think not. After all, Claudine and Colette's most over-the-top moments were personal ones. Claudine is as extravagant and self-indulgent walking alone through the streets of Paris in search of the country life and the childhood she's lost as when she's brilliantly drunk on sparkling wine. That daring leads her to eavesdropping and ill-timed outbursts, failed affairs and forbidden ones, and we are left with the feeling that while surely there's a time and a place for self-restraint, love and self-respect are no place for the bit and the reins.

In a media landscape so cluttered with ego and false courage, it's hard to find true extravagance among the poseurs. Colette would have laughed at and loved our Madonnas and Lady Gagas, with their provocative commitment to pushing the envelope for scandal's sake. True self-indulgence becomes even more challenging as we are encouraged to think small, curl up, and protect ourselves in response to scary social and financial forces. Austerity is the code word du jour, but is a heroine really served by constant calculation and levelheadedness? The knack must be in finding some kind of balance between outrageous action and cautious thought. Elusive and often out of reach, balance is a skill neither Claudine nor Colette ever really mastered.

There's something so fresh and appealing about Claudine's imperfections that it becomes easier to tolerate my own. After all, aren't the qualities that make Claudine so human precisely the ones that move her toward happiness? It would be different if she were all play and no seriousness, but Colette made sure to give her heroine a heart that restlessly seeks love and recognition and a head that knows when she's gone too far. For women who will never be chastened for refusing to properly restrain our feminine hair or for daring to enjoy ourselves in bed, it can be hard to remember that Claudine's small indulgences were important ones. The Paris of Colette's day was resolutely libertine, but it was also one in which wives still belonged to their husbands and daughters to their fathers. Claudine and Colette's insistence on enjoying themselves takes on even more significance when we stop to consider how hard that may have been to accomplish. And Colette's claim to the literary credit she deserved was just as daring as her most profligate romantic feats.

I'll admit it, after I discovered the Claudine novels I walked around with a sly new sense of possibility, a desire to push up against the boundaries I don't always acknowledge around me. I may not have wanted to go out and seduce someone inappropriate, but I definitely wanted to pause and enjoy my body and my mind, to seek out pleasure for a moment even in an unpleasant time. Part of the power of Colette is her insistence that, no matter how doomed a love affair or hopelessly cloistered a life, an indulgent enjoyment of what pleasure we can create for ourselves is our right and our due. That's something a heroine can carry around with her even if she knows she'll be credited with every word she writes. Informed by the spirit, if not the letter, of Claudine's teenage rebellion, a heroine can claim what's hers, no matter who tells her it's off-limits. And she can take a Colette-like pleasure in kicking life's Willys to the curb.

We remember Colette as one of life's more indulgent figures not because she shied away from her due, but because she pursued it even when life threw heartbreak, intrigue, infidelity, lost love, and war in her path. Any heroine on the verge of claiming that life for herself will be accompanied by Colette and outrageous Claudine. After all, aren't heroines called upon to rise higher than the petty concerns that threaten to tether them? Is it even possible to author a life as deliciously scandalous as theirs? I, for one, would love to find out.

READ THIS BOOK:

- When you're as nervous and claustrophobic as a country cat forced to live in a small city apartment
- When you tire of changing your hairstyle as a mode of rebellion and are looking for some daring inspiration
- Over café au lait and a croissant at your favorite coffee shop

CLAUDINE'S LITERARY SISTERS:

- Linda Radlett in *The Pursuit of Love*, by Nancy Mitford
- Nancy Astley in *Tipping the Velvet*, by Sarah Waters
- The nameless main character of *The Lover*, by Marguerite Duras

CHAPTER 7

FIGHT

Scarlett O'Hara in *Gone With the Wind,* by Margaret Mitchell

> Fighting is like champagne. It goes to the heads
> of cowards as quickly as of heroes. Any fool can
> be brave on a battlefield when it's be brave or
> else be killed.

MARGARET MITCHELL, *GONE WITH THE WIND*

Margaret "Peggy" Mitchell was in fighting form, surrounded by dilapidated manila envelopes, which, stacked up, nearly made it to the top of her barely-five-feet-in-high-heels frame. Earlier that day, she'd been a smiling and enthusiastic hostess. But now the sweet woman that had ushered the literary scout Harold Latham around Atlanta had been replaced by an impulsive spitfire. Her eyes snapped as she held out a piece of her gargantuan manuscript. "Take it before I change my mind," she said. She did change her mind, but not before Latham had been seared by the book she had given him. By then it was too late: her fight had unleashed a literary phenomenon, and all because a snide friend had doubted her ability to write.

When asked to show Latham around Atlanta in April 1935, Peggy reluctantly agreed. Once she was roped into the task, though, it just wasn't in her nature to deny a perfect stranger all the hospitality a Southerner could muster. She took him from social event to social event, introducing him to everyone she knew, charming him with the dexterity of an experienced hostess. When Latham implied that she herself might have something juicy to show him, she tried to hide her impatience. No, no, she dissembled; she was just an ex-journalist, not a novelist. But then the forces of literary history struck, delivering an insult that would change the course of Peggy's life forever. A sharp-tongued friend overheard and interjected, her voice laced with sarcasm. Peggy had written a novel, she said, though she wasn't sure how someone as frivolous as Margaret Mitchell could have much to say about anything at all.

Peggy laughed along with the others, but inside she was seething. When she finished dropping off Latham, she catapulted around her apartment, looking under desks and inside closets for the piles of manuscript she'd been accumulating for the last ten years. The manila envelopes had been hidden under towels, used as footrests and coasters and doorstops. They were coffee-stained and discolored with age, some still sporting handwritten notes to self. Now they were thrown into the car. When she finished handing them off to Latham, she was overcome with relief and a bit of fear: maybe this time she had gone a bit too far.

But Peggy was used to a rousing fight. It seemed she'd been on the offensive since before she formed her first coherent memories, for though her life had followed the simple trajectory of a Georgia debutante for the most part, her boisterous insides had never really matched the polite Southern girl she was supposed to portray. Atlanta, Georgia, was a place where name was everything, where a girl acted and thought like other girls if she wished to stay afloat. Externally, Peggy managed to be everything that was expected of her: gracious, inviting, a good conversationalist, and an expert flatterer. But the tiny body that obediently danced, sat, and played along concealed a defiant, unruly mind.

She inherited some of her uppiteness from her mother, Maybelle, a suffragist who warned her not to give over her life to that of some man. "Give of yourself with both hands and overflowing heart," she wrote to Peggy just days before her death of Spanish influenza in 1918, "but give only the excess after you have lived your life." Peggy had struggled with her mother's unflappable sense of authority and her unerring knack for knowing just what to do; now she tussled with her advice. Ultimately, she defied it. Once her mother was gone, she had a chance to take the helm of a respectable Southern family, even if it meant leaving college and taking on the dull social duties expected of a matriarch. She snatched up the opportunity, never suspecting it would be one of her life's first battles.

Peggy knew that any brainy girl could win the battle of Society, with a capital *S*, so long as she had cute clothing, a knack for conversation, and a whole lot of gumption. She possessed all these things, but that didn't mean that managing the role left so empty by her mother's death came easily. Not only did she have to oversee the upkeep of a large house for her father and brother, two men unused to any kind of tumult, but she had to tackle a social landscape fraught with suspicious matrons, gossiping "friends," and plenty of men. The latter were a battle she rushed to fight and conquer, prevailing again and again. She was quick to assemble her own army of slobbering suitors, men who hung around her house dejectedly, called constantly, barraged her with unwanted correspondence, even crowded around her sickbed when she was in the hospital. These were men who hung on her every breathless, flattering word. And juggling their affections was just about the easiest thing she faced in the years that followed.

Already an outsider due to religion (her mother was a devout Catholic), a Northern education at Smith College, and a socially inept grandmother who didn't care about her powerful enemies, Peggy struggled for acceptance in Atlanta. It would have helped if she'd actually cared what anyone thought of her, but that was one part of playing along she just couldn't fake. Small in stature but long on personality, she struggled to embrace her role as sweet little debutante. Women had won the vote, but they weren't encouraged to express their own opinions, of which Peggy had many. Bored by her constant battles to fit in, she began to act out.

The Roaring Twenties suited Peggy perfectly. She took her newfound flapper role to heart, scandalizing her elders and getting the papers talking along the way. That in and of itself was a novelty: women were supposed to shy away from overt publicity as they would a leering rapist or a muddy gutter. But Peggy embraced, even encouraged, the newspapers' interest in her dubious relationships and wild habits. 1921 may have marked Peggy's uncertain debut into society, but she did far more than attend balls and appear at community service events. The exclamation point to the new debutante's hell-raising year was a performance of the violently sexual Apache dance at a ball. Soon, she had added "banned from the Junior League" to her flapper résumé. Next stop: marrying against her father's will. Red Upshaw was dangerous, erratic, and, as it later turned out, violent. He was also handsome and rakish, just the kind of man Peggy was attracted to, and just the person to save her from the oppressive boredom she already associated with Atlanta high society.

Her new marriage was far from boring, but that wasn't a good thing. Red couldn't hold down a job, and his violence and provocation prompted constant arguments. To top it off, he was a bootlegger and rum-runner, a fact that mortified Peggy. She had married to escape; now she was as trapped as she had been at the head of the table in her father's home, where the miserable couple had been encouraged to set up housekeeping. Sick of appeasing her inconsistent husband, she opted for full-out warfare, and writing was her first offensive. She landed her first freelance newspaper writing gig at a local newspaper, her flamboyant byline of "Peggy Mitchell" deliberately making no mention of her married name.

This flagrant provocation hit its mark. After revelations of the extent of Red's illegal activities, it became clear that the marriage was over. Now separated, Peggy moved to her next battle: becoming a woman journalist in a town that banned women from most newspaper offices. Somehow, she fast-talked her way into a job at the *Atlanta Journal*. Peggy ignored the crudity of the language that surrounded her at the offices of the *Journal*, brushed away the cigarette butts that surrounded her, and got to work sniffing out stories in places unfit for any lady. Blasé about her dislike for proofreading and her inability to use a typewriter, she went on to get daring interviews with generals, ax murderers, and even Rudolph Valentino.

That she held her own was no small feat. That she did so while under constant physical threat from her ex-husband, who at one point beat her so severely she was hospitalized, was even more impressive. She slept with a gun at her side through those years and put on a brave front. But inside, the constant danger was taking its toll. She started to have medical problems and accidents that were exacerbated by her nervous temperament and her propensity toward hardship and struggle. She tried to ward off her failing health and spirits by marrying Red's former best man, *Journal* proofreader John Marsh, but even he couldn't protect her from the mysterious ailments that began to encroach on her life and her comfort. Beaten for the time being, she retired from the newspaper business and took to her bed.

Never a model patient, Peggy was a wretched, cranky invalid. Her irritability inevitably got her into trouble. First she read all of the books adoring John could provide her, exhausting the riches of the local library and then the surrounding colleges and universities before reaching an impasse that could not be filled by medical tomes, pornography, or popular literature. Annoyed, she took her husband's advice and propped herself up with a ream of paper and a typewriter to draft the last chapter of a novel about the Civil War. She'd later insist that the decision to start with the end and work back to the beginning was just an old ambulance-chasing journalist's habit. But what Peggy had begun to envision couldn't fit into a newspaper. She was already embroiled in a book that could only be called "epic."

Nobody will ever know how long it took Peggy to draft and edit *Gone With the Wind*. She certainly never told, just as she never discussed the book with her family or friends while she was writing it. This obsessive need to control her public image was matched only by the relentless drive with which she wrote. Her manuscript piled up all over the tiny apartment called "The Dump" by one and all. Said apartment was full of friends, phone calls, and visitors, distractions that made her cagier and crazier the further she got into her dense narrative. Everyone knew about the book soon enough, but nobody could get any details out of Peggy. She laughed when they teased her about writing "the great American novel," changing the subject as quickly as possible.

Inside, though, she was occupied with much more than the creation of a really long book. *Gone With the Wind* was part of Peggy's lifelong struggle to make sense of a tradition-bound world that expected her to content herself with her family name and her deft grasp of Southern customs. A dual narrative of a defeated way of life and an undefeatable heroine, it covers massive territory, weaving together birth and death, family ties, and fatal historical forces. Appropriately, Scarlett's story plays out against a historical backdrop as complex and contradictory as its heroine, a woman whose internal battles are as violent as any Appomattox. At its core, the book is about the one thing Peggy knew best of all: fight.

Scarlett O'Hara is more than painfully self-serving. She's a heroine who gets under the skin like that seductive splinter you can't quite remove. Where perfect heroines are brave, she is weak; where they act with decision, she is fickle and mercurial. She wastes a lifetime of love on a harebrained obsession with a man of inaction, brutalizes her offspring, and throws away the affection of everyone who counts. And still we read and reread *Gone With the Wind*, as obsessed with Scarlett's fight for her land, her life, and her ridiculous love as she is with her own survival.

Peggy's exhaustive depiction of Civil War battles is nothing next to Scarlett's smaller war on her own behalf. Unsuited for anything but luxury, Scarlett is the last person we'd expect to hike up her skirts and deliver a baby or schlep her hated sister-in-law, Melanie Wilkes, over miles of gutted terrain. But Scarlett is a warrior, if not always a particularly likable one. When backed into a corner, she fights for her life, dragging anyone and everyone along with her to epic effect.

Rumor has it that Margaret Mitchell wrote the scenes in which Scarlett survives the siege of Atlanta in one marathon sitting, and I for one have never been able to put them down, preferring instead to let myself be pulled along by Scarlett's terror-fueled flight to Tara at the peril of my own appointments, meals, and bedtimes. I've inhaled the book again and again, from my first stint as a sixth-grader pressed up against a musty bus seat to my days as a relatively cosmopolitan woman cramped into commercial flights and solo lunches, but time and experience haven't dulled the impact of Peggy's ragged, unstoppable narrative. There's something so cruel and vital about Scarlett's fight that I can't help but watch it, jaw ajar with the same awe inspired by an erupting volcano or a mudslide that threatens to take down Malibu.

But train-wreck voyeurism isn't the only thing that makes Scarlett an unforgettable heroine. It's easy to identify with her brief battle against the teachings of childhood, values that just don't fit into a world full of maggots and starvation and $300 mortgages. As we watch Scarlett change from a girl who idolizes her gentle mother's every action to a hard woman who would sell her body to save the farm, there's an icky sense of identification. Who among us hasn't had to reexamine something she thought was important when the stakes were high enough? And who among us hasn't hurt someone else in the pursuit of her own goals?

Rhett Butler has it right when he points out that Scarlett's never as appealing as when she's backed into a corner. We can't help but cheer her on, even as she steals her sister's fiancé, shoots a Yankee in the face, and underestimates the love that surrounds her despite all odds. And we can't help but envy her knack for dismissing risk when it is inconvenient to her, looking instead to a fictitious tomorrow that we know will never come:

> "I won't think of that now," she said firmly. "If I think of it now, it will upset me. There's no reason why things won't come out the way I want them—if he loves me. And I know he does!"
>
> She raised her chin and her pale, black-fringed eyes sparkled in the moonlight. Ellen had never told her that desire and attainment were two different matters; life had not taught her that the race was not to the swift. She lay in the silvery shadows with courage rising and made the plans that a sixteen-year-old makes when life has been so pleasant that defeat is an impossibility and a pretty dress and a clear complexion are weapons to vanquish fate.

Scarlett is nothing if not results-oriented, and she usually gets what she wants. Lacking in self-awareness and psychotically uninterested in the emotions or motivations of others, she uses the tools that have been given her, be they her inner grit or her mother's green curtains. And she does so whether others accept her point of view or not. Even when it tears her up to do what she must do, she shoulders the burden of her life and moves ahead, her decisions swift, self-serving, and without compromise. This blinders-on approach is one of hard offense and unwavering defense, and defeat is not an option. Scary? Yes. Effective? Very.

Scarlett and her creator both excelled at the surprise struggle, the kind of conflict that arises when you're looking the other way. To say that Peggy Mitchell was blindsided by the success of *Gone With the Wind*, which was immediately purchased by an enthusiastic Latham, would be a gross understatement. The book she almost withheld from the world sparked a revolution in publishing, a Pulitzer Prize, worldwide translations, a movie adaptation phenomenon, and a lifetime spent swatting away gossiping relations and fame-chasing fans. Characteristically, Peggy took to this battle, shoring up her defenses and drawing her boundaries very carefully around herself. In later years, she fought for her privacy just as hard as she battled for fame, withstanding lifelong criticism of her pulpy literary methods, her racism, and her unschooled literary style. And while *Gone With the Wind* is nothing if not racist, manipulative, and pulpy, it's a book I can't quite be ashamed of reading and rereading. Can I really be expected to push against the boundaries of my own life without a bit of inspiration from literature's most lovable bitch?

It would be easy to discard Scarlett in favor of the woman Peggy always claimed was "the real heroine" of *Gone With the Wind*, but I can't see Melanie Wilkes gaining a cult following any time soon. Sure, she's practical and saintly and dear, but she lacks the fire and impatience that make Scarlett so maddening and so marvelously brave. Where Melanie lays down her arms, Scarlett takes them up with twice as much vigor. And though Melanie is able to create happiness all around her, a heroine's trait if ever I've seen one, her happiness will always lack the Technicolor clarity of the few joyful moments Scarlett allows herself.

As a modern-day heroine struggling for boring things like work-life balance and exciting ones like self-definition and -esteem, I'm always better served when I let others join me in the fight. Scarlett and Peggy both pushed others away to the detriment of their success and happiness; Scarlett, at least, pays a heavy price for her unwillingness to let others into her life. As I revisit *Gone With the Wind* as an adult woman, I'm shocked at the community Scarlett so selfishly discards, throwing away Melanie's and Rhett's unconditional love in favor of a hypothetical and ill-fated emotional bond.

But even through my disdain of Scarlett's selfishness, I am reminded that a heroine's most serious battles are often fought alone. Scarlett's steely exterior hides a woman who must choose to either live inside the pain of insecurity and thwarted love or move through it. We all know which option she chooses, and we all can learn from her spectacular defeat. Her blatant willingness to leave her heart behind in favor of the battle itself is, perhaps, her greatest weakness. And I, at least, can't help but afford it my grudging admiration, as Ashley does when Scarlett decides to put aside her emotions in favor of survival:

He remembered the way she had squared her shoulders when she turned away from him that afternoon, remembered the stubborn lift of her head. His heart went out to her, torn with his own helplessness, wrenched with admiration. He knew she had no such word in her vocabulary as gallantry, knew she would have stared blankly if he had told her she was the most gallant soul he had ever known. He knew she would not understand how many truly fine things he ascribed to her when he thought of her as gallant. He knew that she took life as it came, opposed her tough-fibered mind to whatever obstacles there might be, fought on with a determination that would not recognize defeat, and kept on fighting even when she saw defeat was inevitable.

But, for four years, he had seen others who had re-fused to recognize defeat, men who rode gaily into sure disaster because they were gallant. And they had been defeated, just the same.

He thought as he stared at Will in the shadowy hall that he had never known such gallantry as the gal-lantry of Scarlett O'Hara going forth to conquer the world in her mother's velvet curtains and the tail feathers of a rooster.

READ THIS BOOK:

- When the mortgage payment is (over)due
- Whenever your personal Melanie Wilkes thwarts your self-centered plans
- At the hotel you've spirited yourself away to for a secret, selfish staycation

SCARLETT'S LITERARY SISTERS:

- Any heroine in *The Portable Dorothy Parker*, by Dorothy Parker
- Christabel LaMotte and Maud Bailey in *Possession*, by A. S. Byatt
- Lily Bart in *The House of Mirth*, by Edith Wharton

CHAPTER 8

COMPASSION

Scout Finch in *To Kill a Mockingbird*, by Harper Lee

"An' they chased him 'n' never could catch him 'cause they didn't know what he looked like, an' Atticus, when they finally saw him, why he hadn't done any of those things . . . Atticus, he was real nice. . . ."

"Most people are, Scout, when you finally see them."

HARPER LEE, *TO KILL A MOCKINGBIRD*

A girl may be born with grit, faith, or happiness, but compassion is an advanced heroine skill, one that's usually drummed into you by circumstance, life, and error. It's one of those qualities that's easier to understand once you've collected a bruise or two, something that comes with practice, not will. It helps to be an outsider like Nelle Harper

Lee, a woman who learned her compassion while filling a permanent seat on the sidelines of Southern life.

Monroeville, Alabama, did not place a high premium on compassion or modernity or anything, for that matter, but tradition. Even in the 1930s, the town had barely managed to embrace electricity. For Nelle, its streets were as familiar as the flour sacks from which her poor classmates' clothing was made, its pace as slow as a wound-down metronome.

Nelle learned about the sidelines in her awkward role as the tomboy who clashed with her parents and could never really fit in at school. The fact that she had taken Truman Streckfus Persons, an effeminate neighbor boy, under her wing when she was eight years old did not help. Both were destined to become literary legends, Harper as a literary enigma and Truman Capote as the enfant terrible of American letters. But for the time being, they were a weird, ugly little couple, occupying the farthest outskirts of school society.

Life at home had little of the uproarious fun she manufactured with Truman. Nelle had to watch her father, Amasa "A. C." Lee, deal with her mother as she progressed from sickly to downright mentally ill. Every inch the upright country lawyer, A. C. passed on his love of learning and reading to Nelle. Best of all, he gave her a typewriter, a gift upon which she and Truman promptly skewered the collective Monroeville populace in a series of thinly veiled romans à clef. But for all her bookish proclivities, Harper was no shut-in. She played football (tackle over touch) and fought for Truman's honor when he was harassed (fists over insults). She knew that eventually she'd have to follow in the footsteps of her sacrificing sister Alice, whom she lovingly called "Bear." Dutiful and enterprising, Alice had pleased her father by getting her law degree. Nelle, too, idolized A. C., and she knew that following her sister's lead would help repay her father for the years of care and single parenting he had given them so willingly.

But when Nelle got to the University of Alabama, she was on the sidelines once more. She just couldn't act like her proper, ladylike classmates. A gangly disaster in a sea of marriage-obsessed robots, she tried desperately to liven things up a bit. But her swearing, smoking, and racy conversation couldn't cover up the truth: she hated the law. When she quit law school, she felt like a double disappointment, abandoning both her family business and her home. Nelle was moving on and out.

She set her sights on New York City and life as a writer. But Manhattan was a cruel shock to her system. The city, teeming with postwar life, hardly had any vacant apartments, let alone jobs. She contented herself with a cold-water flat and a job in a bookstore. But though she made some friends, she came no closer to her goal of breaking into publishing. Her ongoing struggle must have made what happened next even more incredible. When she finally landed a literary agent, her friends responded with an extraordinary gift. On Christmas Day 1956, her friends Michael and Joy Brown, a composer and ballerina she befriended during her time in New York, gave her a check for a year's worth of living expenses, accompanied by a simple card that read, "You have one year off from your job to write whatever you please. Merry Christmas."

Aware of the import of a gift that came from a place of generosity and love, Nelle focused all of her attention on what she would later call a love story, plain and simple. Writing *To Kill a Mockingbird* wasn't easy; in fact, in interviews given after the book was published, Nelle intimated that writing it was almost akin to torture. She rewrote the book at least three times during that year, which she later described as "a hopeless time." And with good reason: writing the book required her to walk back down the streets of Monroeville in her mind, looking for clues to the worst life had to offer.

As notoriously reclusive as J. D. Salinger or Carson Mc-

Cullers, Harper Lee hasn't told us much about her first and only book aside from what she placed so lovingly in its pages. Though the book is widely recognized as autobiographical, Nelle herself has declined to point out the line between fiction and reality. As curious readers, we're forced to look into what we know of her childhood for answers.

Like the place where she formed her first opinions and impressions, fictitious Maycomb is a town that's comatose on the outside, simmering and seething within. Inhabited by Christians and patriotic Alabamans, it's a place where white townsfolk tolerate, even encourage, racism and segregation; where white and black only mingle in carefully coordinated boss-servant relationships. In Maycomb, black women raise white children with love and forbearance; there, too, all whites know that blacks are a dirty footnote in the history of a region wronged by war and poverty. Everyone, that is, except for Jean Louise "Scout" Finch, a six-year-old girl who is too young to know better.

Scout is more than a heroine—she's a stand-in for her mysterious author. Like Nelle, she stands firmly on the sidelines, marginalized by age and parentage. She's a child, a grouchy, energetic thing, a kid whose skinned knees and bleached-out hair are as easy to imagine as her squirmy countenance. She is also the daughter of Atticus Finch, a

small-town lawyer whose obsession with truth and tolerance will unravel all of Maycomb's drowsy comfort in one
tumultuous summer. Over the course of the book, Scout
becomes our guide through the pain of children confront-
ing the gory, terrifying realities of adulthood.

Again and again, Scout's reality is altered; again and
again she brings her questions to lay on Atticus's shoulders.
Scout, her brother Jem, and their neighbor Dill repeatedly
see things they are not meant to see: conversations between
their father and a mob intent on vigilante justice; a trial with
undertones of incest, rape, and racism. Their encounters
with the dark world of adults are full of mystery and unan-
swered questions for Atticus, who must bear the weight not
just of the trial but of its moral and ethical repercussions.
The book's portrayal of Atticus's struggle is in itself a work
of compassion on the part of Harper, who watched her own
father grapple with complex questions of right and wrong
during her childhood, including the time he unsuccessfully
defended two black men accused of murder. Shattered by
his failure, he never took on another criminal case.

But to mistake Atticus for A. C. would be to miss the point
entirely. Nelle's father was a man with his own demons, one
who was very slow to adopt the racial tolerance that would
be the mark of his literary heir. Instead, I see Atticus as

Nelle's way of thanking her father for the moral compass he instilled in her and for his years of protection and care. Atticus is what every child needs: a parent who is loved and who embodies love for his children. And Scout needs Atticus more than ever when her childhood life tilts and falters.

Scout's significance as a heroine lies in her willingness to rethink what she *thinks* she knows. Boo Radley is a terrifying monster . . . right? So how come he delivers gifts to the kids? How can an ill-tempered and irascible old woman also be a human like anyone else, battling for freedom from an ugly addiction? How can Scout and Jem reconcile the Atticus they know to be a good and honest father as the man who is held up as a "nigger-lover" and someone to be feared? Scout must rethink the pillars of her childhood until its foundations are as dug-up as Miss Maudie's blackened, burned-out cellar.

"You never really understand a person until you consider things from his point of view—until you climb into his skin and walk around in it," Atticus tells his little girl. It's the little girl who remembers those words and dares to hold the mirror of her character to reflect our own attitudes, values, and truths. Once Scout learns to think from goblinlike Boo's point of view, she finds love, not fear. In a sea change for Scout and the book, she begins to trust someone else's actions instead of what she's been told to think about him. This act—the courage to view another with compassion, to trust the person instead of the myth—is the end of childhood, but it's the beginning of an under-standing adulthood. And, in an echo of her own lessons from her father, Harper delivers our own awakening through the mouth of an unconventional, rowdy, rude, and feisty little girl with a lot of growing up to do.

If understanding, then, is the beginning of compas-sion, compassion breeds courage for Scout. The girl who'd defend her daddy's name in a split second learns to take a deep breath and reconsider. Armed with her newfound knowledge about the nature of things, she takes another look at the people, places, and traditions she's always taken for granted. Seen through another lens, Maycomb's Mrs. Duboses turn from crotchety old women to addicts strug-gling for independence and peace. For every supposedly polite resident who turns out to be bad, there is a bad one like Dolphus Raymond who turns out to be good. The rev-elation that his reprehensible-looking bag of moonshine actually contains Coca-Cola is a surprise straight from the wit of the wise Harper Lee, who thinks a heroine's preju-dices and preconceived notions ought to be riled up every once in a while.

For me, Scout's most poignant moments aren't the ones in which she learns new lessons; they're the ones in which she's a reckless, school-hating little kid, a girl who'd rather hike up her britches and look hard at a bug than wear skirts and act nice. Scout's not ornery for orneriness' sake; she's herself at all times. She puts a face on what things like racism and intolerance can do to a town, to a country, and to a person. Seen through the eyes of a child, the injustices of Maycomb become even more unacceptable. It's hard to stomach brash intolerance in others when a small child is able to spot it and question it in herself. As women given a walk in the shoes of Scout, we must ask ourselves what we are willing to let our children and our daughters see. Whenever I put down *To Kill a Mockingbird*, it's with an almost sick feeling of mixed despair and wild, klutzy hope. Simple to read, it's not too easy to digest. Maybe that's the point.

Harper Lee sure used her year off well. *To Kill a Mockingbird* won a Pulitzer Prize after its publication in 1960, but the sweetness of this award was complicated by a literary betrayal a few years later on the part of her childhood friend Truman, whom she had helped to write *In Cold Blood* and who didn't even include her in the acknowledgments. *To Kill a Mockingbird* made her famous, all right, but the book endured constant challenges in schools and public libraries. At first she tried to keep up with the deluge, doing her best to answer the letters, calls, and interview requests that poured in for America's most sought-after author. But slowly she became content to trade places with her little heroine, taking off for the sidelines again and letting Scout do the talking.

It can feel a bit weird to speculate about Harper Lee's true intentions using only her book and none of her biography. Who are we to peek into a life so carefully held private? Nelle's mysterious nature, though, is an opportunity for a heroine eager to flex those new compassion muscles. When we step into her shoes and think from her vantage point, it's easy to see why she'd send such a powerful heroine out into the world in her stead. For Scout and what she symbolizes is bigger than Nelle Harper Lee or any one of us.

To Kill a Mockingbird is still a cultural touchstone; years after its appearance, Demi Moore even named her daughter Scout, and our schools still consider the book required reading. Sure, segregation ended long ago, but the decline of overt racism in our society will always be accompanied by new injustices, new chances for a heroine to practice compassion toward others. Intimidated, perhaps, by our culture's chew-'em-up-and-spit-'em-out approach to literary celebrity, Harper Lee has chosen to remain silent on the impact of her groundbreaking work. It's a good thing her book more than stands on its own.

As heroines, it's easy to shy away from the sidelines and difficult to respect another person's place there. The sidelines are a liminal place and a downright weird one. In order to live there, you have to give up the option of defending yourself with words or actions and simply allow others to see you as they will. For some, the sidelines aren't a choice at all; they're a place where people are forced by custom or hatred, intolerance and poverty. They're the place where poor, plain people live, people who are doomed to the margins of society and who know what it's like to be down and out. But it's there, standing right alongside Harper Lee, that the Boos and Scouts live, too, the people whom we cannot afford to overlook or abandon.

Compassion is a heroine's courage to look over there, too, to recognize the parts of others and of herself that are consigned to endless side-spaces and see what she finds. As Scout discovers, taking things at face value can help maintain a certain semblance of peace for a while, but it can also endanger your very life. When we choose status quo over the truth, we fail to act heroically. When we choose judgment over compassion, we allow the loud ones, the Stephanie Crawfords and the Ewells and those who would allow an innocent man to die for the color of his skin, to prevail. It's hard to choose the rougher route, the one that promises to disrupt everything that's quiet and serene inside ourselves and then delivers with abandon. But the alternative is chilling. When we adopt the tactics of ignorance that are the easy way out, looking the other way instead of acting from compassion, we fail everyone on the sidelines. Like it or not, when we fail to at least attempt to practice compassion, we fail ourselves as well.

Like her heroic little girl, Harper Lee herself had a soft spot in her heart for the people on the outskirts, and part of the power of her only published book is that she always includes their whispers among the shouts of the self-righteous and powerful. Her heart was always with those people branded as insignificant or difficult, and in a 1965 speech she said, "Our response to these people represents our earthly test. And I think that these people enrich the wonder of our lives. It is they who most need our kindness, because they seem less deserving. After all, anyone can love people who are lovely."

READ THIS BOOK:

- Before you go to court or have to stare down a
  particularly loathsome work project
- With your own little girl
- When you get tired of being yelled at by cable news

SCOUT'S LITERARY SISTERS:

- Daisy Fay Harper in *Daisy Fay and the Miracle Man*,
  by Fannie Flagg
- Lily Owens in *The Secret Life of Bees*, by Sue Monk
  Kidd
- Meg Murry in *A Wrinkle in Time*, by Madeleine
  L'Engle

CHAPTER 9

SIMPLICITY

Laura Ingalls in *The Long Winter*, by Laura Ingalls Wilder

I am beginning to learn that it is the sweet, simple things of life which are the real ones after all.

LAURA INGALLS WILDER,

"A BOUQUET OF WILD FLOWERS"

"Are we there yet? Is this the prairie?" I looked out the window of the Toyota Tercel. We were driving cross-country and I had insisted that my boyfriend take me on a route that at least skirted the prairie lands of the vast Plains states. The trip wouldn't include the sites of Laura Ingalls Wilder's childhood, but it was a pilgrimage of sorts. As we reached Kansas and watched the road flatten into endless, monotonous horizon, I imagined how it must have felt to encounter a land so wild, expansive, and simple in a vehicle far clunkier and more uncomfortable than ours. Though the radio was blaring and my boyfriend was within arm's length, I could feel a sense of quiet set in. After all, there's not much to focus on but your own heartbeat when you're under a vast prairie sky.

Leaning out that car window, I was transported back more than a hundred years to the way in which my childhood friend and mentor, Laura Ingalls Wilder, the woman whose stories of prairie life have meant the world to millions of readers like me, encountered this land for the first time. I looked out at the grassy landscape, deceptive in its size and almost endless in its inscrutable power. I imagined what it must have been like for the tiny Ingalls family, dwarfed by the forces of nature around them, as they traveled west to make their home in a new country. And even I, connoisseur of historical fiction and professional imaginer of other places and times, found it hard to conceive of a landscape completely stripped of modern accouterments.

Not that I hadn't tried. It seems that simplicity becomes more and more desirable as daily life gets more complex. All around us are confusing subprime mortgages, 401(k) statements, crowded closets, and complicated living arrangements, things that make us want to take shelter under the simple quilt of yesteryear. Modern life has backfired a bit, it seems, stripping us of our autonomy, leaving us dependent and discontented even as we luxuriate in a standard of living unknown to our forebears. Lucky for us, it's fashionable to slough off worldly things in the name of conscience. We're not alone in seeking a simpler reality, one that focuses on people instead of things and gives honor to who we are as people without burying us under the stuff that can obscure reality as quickly as a storm cloud on the prairie.

These weren't exactly worries shared by Laura and her family. They had an important role to play in westward expansion and the civilization of a rough land, hewing a productive nation from the vast and endless physical landscape that exhilarated and terrified young Laura. In short, they had bigger concerns: fires had to be built by dint of fuel they gathered themselves; clothing had to be stretched to the last stitch, twice-turned and mended, and then put to further use in quilts, aprons, or curtains.

In Laura's world, there were no leftovers or seconds. When they left the little house near Independence, Kansas, the Ingallses even dug up the seed potatoes growing in their garden. Every physical possession was something precious, but not necessarily vital. What they could not buy, they traded for crops or furs. Glass windows, bathrooms, and swift transportation are fundamental necessities to us, but they were luxuries to a people who produced almost everything they needed themselves, relying only peripherally on items purchased at far-away stores. As a result, Laura's family was fiercely independent and self-confident, answering the call of western expansion again and again as they made their own mark on the frontier.

Laura's life may have been simple in terms of material possessions, but it wasn't easy. The years following her marriage to Almanzo Wilder were fraught with trouble. At first, all signs pointed to a happy, unruffled marriage. Almanzo, whom Laura called Manly, was a successful farmer and horse breeder with rich relatives, and Laura was an adept housekeeper and a smart manager used to deprivation and simple living. But nothing could have prepared the newlyweds for the disastrous years that lay ahead. Almanzo fell ill with diphtheria, forcing a long separation from their young daughter Rose and partially paralyzing him for the remainder of his life. The couple's next child, a boy, died before he was a month old; their house burned down; and a drought dried up any hopes of financial prosperity. The couple moved around in a futile search for land that could sustain them, taking on odd jobs as they went and raising Rose with a sense of constant inferiority and poverty.

Eventually, the Wilders moved to Rocky Ridge Farm

in Mansfield, Missouri, forcing its unforgiving terrain into submission over many long years of toil and labor. By the time Laura was moved to write about her childhood, the hard years were finally over, and the couple had been living in relative security, if not full financial bloom, for years. Rose was a successful writer who traveled the world; even Laura wrote regularly as a columnist on poultry farming and rural life for the *Missouri Ruralist*.

It wasn't until the onset of the increasingly dire circumstances of the Great Depression that Laura really began thinking about simpler times. There was something familiar about this new era of poverty and uncertainty, something that resonated with the Ingallses' own roving years. Laura's family had never had much, but they had always managed to eke out a slight living and stay together. This courage and tenacity seemed especially suited to Depression-era life, with its privations and pressing needs. It had been years since Laura saw such widespread unemployment, hunger, and want. Now, combined with her mother's death, these reduced circumstances made her look backward to the experiences of her pioneer childhood. Laura, who was in her early sixties, began to write a memoir she called *Pioneer Girl*, a first-person manuscript detailing her family's westward journey. In 1930, she showed the book to her journalist daughter for her opinion, and before she knew it, Laura was adapting passages for a children's book tentatively titled *When Grandma Was a Little Girl*.

It can be easy to confuse the real Laura with the Laura of her books, to mistake the Little House on the Prairie series for a sweet tale of churning butter and stomping on hay. At the time of their publication, nobody had ever really undertaken what Laura achieved with such success: a series of books aimed at children that re-created a historical period in such vivid and compelling detail. Succeed she did, but not by telling life exactly as it was. In fact, the books were written over thirteen contentious, uneasy years marked by a decidedly complex relationship with her grown daughter, Rose Wilder Lane. Though Rose's role in the creation of the Little House books has gained acknowledgment in recent years, many Laura fans have no idea of the degree to which she influenced both the form and success of her mother's—fictitious—life story.

Throughout the process of crafting the book, Laura drew upon her daughter for editorial and moral support. By this time, Rose was a restless, resentful woman still full of memories of the poverty and restriction of childhood and frustrated by what she saw as her mother's lack of literary sophistication. Family ties didn't turn Rose into a permissive editor; in fact, the editorial letters that survive are brutal, reflecting a lack of sympathy for her mother's literary talent guaranteed to leave an acidic taste in fans' mouths. Rose felt compelled to force the work into the literary image of the day; Laura struggled to live up to her daughter's high standards. Mother and daughter both fought to get their version on the page, collaborating and clashing as they gave simultaneous birth to one of literature's great coups.

Unbeknownst to Laura, Rose was committing a sort of literary heresy even as she helped her mother craft her first novel for children. *Little House in the Big Woods* appeared in 1931 to acclaim and good reviews, and Rose's novel *Let the Hurricane Roar* appeared in 1932. An adult novel following the adventures of a couple named Caroline and Charles as they confront the American West (sound familiar?), the book became a best seller. Though some have suggested that the book was another collaboration between Laura and Rose, more recent works have hinted that Laura had no idea Rose was plundering, even plagiarizing, her unpublished memoir for her own gain. However she felt personally about the book, which was a Depression-era success story in itself, Laura remained silent. We'll never know her true feelings on Rose's betrayal, only that she set them aside in favor of her increasing compulsion to continue her life story. She turned her attention to the next book in the series, then the next, creating and re-creating her frontier childhood for a popular audience.

My favorite Little House book has always been *The Long Winter*, which fictionalizes the Ingallses' struggle during the Snow Winter of 1880–81. It's not a cheerful book per se, but you wouldn't be cheerful if you had lived through that winter, either. Plagued by blizzards and cut off from the railroads for a solid five months by blinding snow and perpetual storms, the residents of De Smet, South Dakota, survived temperatures as low as 35 degrees below zero. The tiny prairie town depended on the railroads for supplies and dry goods; both were stuck behind snow drifts for months on end, until the town's residents were forced to eat their seed wheat or starve.

Laura's fictional account of the winter that almost killed her family is deceptively simple. Though the Ingalls family actually had a young married couple with a baby on the way living with them at the time, Laura chose to write about the family as if they'd survived the winter alone and in utter isolation. Her story of survival and basic instinct takes simplicity to a new extreme. With no firewood and no way of going out for supplies, the family must burn straw they twist into little sticks in their stove for warmth. There's no school, no social activity of any kind, just the monotony of survival. Laura and her sisters crowd around the kitchen table and recite their lessons by day; at night, they sing songs and tell stories for entertainment. With nothing but axle grease for lamp oil, they create a makeshift lamp out of a button and some fabric. When they're not studying or entertaining one another, they bend over a coffee mill, grinding seed wheat into flour for the coarse brown bread that sustains them for months.

Even given the nightmarish circumstances it depicts, there's a humanity and a sense of dignity in the pages of *The Long Winter* that made quite an impression on a little girl who had never seen snow. Stripped of any outside landscape and denied the few comforts to which they have become accustomed, the Ingalls family gets down to basics, and the simple task of living takes up most of their time. Their struggle against the elements is one of waiting, but also one of angry confrontation. Though their relationships with one another are severely restrained by the mores and expectations of 1880s ladies and gentlemen, each member of the Ingalls family loses their patience at some point. Even gentle Ma almost breaks under the knowledge that the train will not come until the blizzards stop.

Ma threw up her hands and dropped into a chair. . . .
"Patience?" Ma exclaimed. "Patience! What's *his* patience got to do with it, I'd like to know!"

But even as they momentarily lose control, the Ingalls
family knows it must cling together to survive. When Laura
complains of being tired of brown bread with nothing on
it, Ma is quick to chasten her: "Don't complain, Laura! . . .
Never complain of what you have. Always remember you
are fortunate to have it."

The Ingallses don't have much to be grateful for, but
their focus on small blessings in the face of unthinkable deprivation gives the book its sweetest moments. The family's few possessions and creature comforts are admittedly
small by modern standards, but their relative lack of complaint seems designed to undercut a culture where a throt-
tled Netflix queue or a choppy cell phone connection can
seem like a cosmic misfortune of epic proportions. But the
fact that they have survived together means more than any
material possession or outward congratulations. And their
celebrations focus on the most simple gift of all: the gift of a
heart that beats and lungs that breathe. A book about death
and threat ends up affirming and clarifying simple daily life
under the most extreme of circumstances.

For fourteen-year-old Laura, the book is about more than surviving harsh weather conditions. *The Long Winter* tests her growing spirit, pitting her against those closest to her in a struggle to remain patient and calm and to fulfill what she knows is her duty. Life was surely less complicated in a society in which the rules of success were so clear. Given a sweet disposition, a strong faith, and a womanly manner, a pioneer girl has everything she needs to move forward. But Laura can't or won't fit into that mold. She is challenged by the circumstances around her and by an internal rebellion that constantly threatens the family unit. This struggle to simultaneously belong and break away is all too familiar to anyone who didn't grow up gracefully. And if Laura doesn't exactly learn patience, she learns that her family has what it needs to sustain itself.

Laura the woman was no stranger to privation and insecurity. The *Little House* books she struggled to write did not entirely heal the rifts with her daughter, but they went a long way toward restoring the love and collegiality at the center of their relationship. When she finished writing the series at last, Laura knew she could rest. Her work was done; she had given something far larger than herself to her daughter and to the generations yet to discover a bit of themselves on Laura's own vast, remembered prairie.

For Laura Ingalls Wilder, the Great Depression wasn't a jarring shock. It was a reminder of the simpler, less materialistic days of her childhood, days when one flickering lamp held together a family, outshining her personal desires. After the profligate 1920s, the '30s must have seemed more comfortable to Laura, who struggled with modernity throughout her adult life. Even in her old age, her first impulse when financial difficulty arose was to cut off the electricity to the house. She had lived so long without it that it must have seemed like an easily expendable luxury.

Should modern readers give up every comfort in simplicity's name? Of course not, but a reading of *The Long Winter* is a good reminder not to let mere things interfere with our heroines' duties. For Laura, simplicity was a way of life in which the luxurious always gave way to the essential. Today's heroine has much to learn from a world in which things like heat and food consumed so much time and energy. There just isn't time to worry about bigger houses, better clothing, or fancier job titles when you're trying to figure out how to stretch your meager supplies just one more week. When we focus on people and life instead of material possessions and mere wants, there's not much room for emotional hand-wringing. Instead, there's more space to weigh what we value in our lives and to acknowledge what really counts. For Laura and her family, simplicity meant paring down until the foundations of life—family, freedom, nothing but the nonnegotiables— were laid bare.

If you're like me, you've yearned for simplicity for as long as you can remember. I was a Laura Ingalls–worshipping, bonnet-wearing eight-year-old right around the time when I began to sense that my family wasn't perfect after all, that my teachers were humans and not gods, that my neighborhood was surrounded by crime and poverty, and that we ourselves would never have all or be all that we could. But the same parents I screamed at and railed against were the people who helped me turn my wood-paneled toy wagon into a covered one, who let me go off and find myself even when they disapproved of the means, the destination, and the young woman I flirted with becoming. It's contradictions like these that send a heroine under the comforter with a good book, one that evokes simpler times.

The simple life still has its challenges. Simplicity must coexist with life's shadowy gray areas, those nooks and crannies of imperfection, struggle, and toil designed to drive a heroine mad. Perhaps Laura's own struggle with a complicated family situation and her decidedly complex relationship with comfort, money, and survival drove her to write works that hearken back to a time of simplicity and grace. Even so, her books challenge modern readers with their intolerant, racist depictions of Native Americans and their decidedly conservative bent, yet another example of the murky territory many literary heroines are called to populate.

Thankfully for us, the Little House on the Prairie books far transcend the gentle reminiscences of an old woman, however weathered by the world. The simplicity they evoke has nothing to do with age or time. Hailing from an era we have little hope of ever experiencing or understanding, they reach across history and tap into a universal longing for calm, serenity, space, and simplicity. Like the pioneer girls who came before us, we crave community, human contact, the chance to prove ourselves as we survive our own long winters. It's easy to lose sight of what really counts in a time so taken with material possessions and fickle fortunes, a time when worrying about bank account balances and precarious markets has been prioritized somewhere between waking up in the morning and voting. Luckily, Laura's there to remind us that sometimes all you need is the flicker of a fire and the companionship of those you love. Life is never simple, but we can strive to make it so.

READ THIS BOOK:

- While on road trips, preferably during stops due to inclement weather
- In a warm bathtub
- When you're tempted to buy something you absolutely don't need
- While nursing a finicky baby

LAURA'S LITERARY SISTERS:

- Hattie Brooks in *Hattie Big Sky*, by Kirby Larson
- Ántonia Shimerda in *My Ántonia*, by Willa Cather
- The sisters from Sydney Taylor's *All-of-a-Kind Family*

CHAPTER 10

STEADFASTNESS

Jane Eyre in *Jane Eyre*, by Charlotte Brontë

> I remembered that the real world was wide, and that
> a varied field of hopes and fears, of sensations and
> excitements, awaited those who had the courage to
> go forth into its expanse, to seek real knowledge of
> life amidst its perils.
>
> **CHARLOTTE BRONTË,** *JANE EYRE*

All too often, the lives of authors we love read like a litany of disappointment, grief, and misery. Charlotte Brontë's story is no exception. For the first thirty-two years of her life she was beaten down by circumstance and devastated by failure after failure. She clung to her family, only to see her two elder sisters die of malnutrition and tuberculosis. She attended school and went out into the world, struggling and failing at the only jobs available to her—governess and teacher—so she returned home, and watched her family fall apart before her eyes. And she wrote, only to see her work skewered as coarse, immoral, and unwomanly.

The story of how this plain, poor writer created one of the greatest literary triumphs in the English language is as much about steadfastness as it is about grief. Charlotte's journey from impotence to immortality started in the damp parsonage at Haworth in harsh northern England, where she lived in the company of her eccentric, literary siblings and a distracted father. The wild, unfettered moors were the perfect place for the awkward Brontës, who spent more time wandering through nature and stomping through their tiny living room than associating with their father's congregation. Isolated, soggy, and freezing cold, the house overlooked a graveyard where, in time, nearly everyone who had ever been close to Charlotte would lie buried.

The motherless Brontë girls enjoyed an unusual degree of education at the hands of their gruff curate father, Patrick, who had taken over their upbringing after Maria Brontë's long, slow death from uterine cancer in 1821. Still, as they grew up, the sisters bumped up against the twin barriers of cultural convention and social standing. Poor and lacking in looks and connections, Charlotte was forced to make her way in a world that didn't think much of feminine ability. The results were less than encouraging. Her forays into the world of governessing and teaching flopped. Every time she forged a path away from Haworth, desperate to make a living, she was forced back home when the money ran out and the well of her employers' goodwill ran dry. Deprived of outside stimulus, Charlotte was continually thwarted by disease, lack of funds, and family emergencies. Though she clung to her sisters in the years that followed, she began to turn inward for solace.

When faced with the vagaries of a world they never cared much to understand, the Brontës wrote. Together with her brother, Branwell, and sisters Emily and Anne, Charlotte was obsessed with violent struggles in imaginary kingdoms throughout her childhood and adolescence. Huddled around the fire of the parsonage, the siblings wrote epic poems and long sagas. But it was the first real personal crisis of her life that prompted Charlotte to write for herself, by herself.

In retrospect, it's amazing that Charlotte had a chance for any kind of failed love at all, obscured as she was by the isolation of Haworth and the lowliness of her own social standing. Still, she managed to fall in love during her year at a boarding school in Brussels . . . and to be deeply wounded when her passion for a married man was first ignored, then roundly rejected. The trip to Brussels was an experiment intended to arm Charlotte with the tools she'd need to open her own school for girls in England. But the expedition took an unexpected turn when she met Constantin Heger, the school's headmaster. Sarcastic, dark, and gruff, Constantin challenged Charlotte's brain as much as her willpower. That challenge lingered as she found herself at home again, depressed and lethargic, gripped with an emotion she hardly dared name.

She tried to distract herself with words, the panacea of her childhood and the only things to which she could entrust her adulterous emotions. At first she could not write at all. Even letters to Heger, whom she begged to contact her, came slowly. "I should not know this lethargy if I could write," she complained. "Otherwise, do you know what I should do, Monsieur? I should write a book, and I should dedicate it to my literature master—to the only master I ever had—to you, Monsieur. . . . But that cannot be. It is not to be thought of. The career of letters is closed to me— only that of teaching is open."

Depressed and listless, maddened by Heger's nonresponse, Charlotte kept turning to her pen. Her struggles slowly unraveled themselves on paper, culminating in a love letter that bleeds with unrequited passion and stifled agony.

"I strove to restrain my tears, to utter no complaint," she wrote. "But when one does not complain, when one seeks to dominate oneself with a tyrant's grip, the faculties start into rebellion and one pays for external calm with an internal struggle that is almost unbearable. Day and night I find neither rest nor peace. If I sleep I am disturbed by tormenting dreams in which I see you. . . . Monsieur, the poor have not need of much to sustain them . . . nor do I, either, need much affection from those I love. . . . But you showed me of yore a little interest . . . and I hold on to the maintenance of that little interest—I hold on to it as I would hold on to life."

He never responded. The letter was later found, torn in pieces and meticulously pieced back together by Heger's wife.

And this is where Charlotte's steadfastness came in. Behind her lay what might have been her only chance at love. In front of her was a future full of bad weather and boredom. Deprived of her beloved professor and doomed to menial chores back at the parsonage, she began to write in earnest.

She wrote about love and deprivation. She wrote poems that blister with isolation and despair. She wrote her first novel. She even wrote one last letter to Heger. She wrote in the living room where she had spun fantastical tales as a child, surrounded by her sisters, who were avid readers and writers. Together, they shivered, worked, and read through the long, dark English winters, taking breaks to pace around the living room. Still, she kept her words to herself.

The orgy of writing that followed was no idyll. The family curse raised its head again as Branwell, once talented and precocious, slid further into the grips of laudanum addiction and alcoholism, humiliating the family with his repeated lapses into debt and his ranting, incoherent behavior. Meanwhile, Emily and Anne were placid and distracted, wrapped up in their own affairs.

Charlotte's jump from literary secrecy to outright ambition was a happy accident. Sometime in late 1845, she picked up one of Emily's notebooks. Idly, she began to read, forgetting that she had not asked permission to do so. What she saw electrified her. "Something more than surprise seized me," she recalled later. "These were not common effusions, nor at all like the poetry women generally write." Forced to confess her perfidy to her sisters, she found herself launching into a heartfelt argument for publication.

It took a while to convince Emily and Anne that publication was desirable or even possible, much less to overcome their scruples over Charlotte's betrayal of Emily's confidence. Anyone else would have given up. But Charlotte knew her sisters, and was convinced that the genius they could demonstrate in words should not lie in state at the parsonage forever. Slowly, she cracked through their reserve, tantalizing them—and herself—with visions of access to a world they could never conquer alone.

Armed with a small legacy from their deceased aunt and uncharacteristically optimistic about their prospects, the trio paid to publish their poems under a set of ambiguous pseudonyms. *Poems by Currer, Ellis, and Acton Bell* appeared in May 1846. Encouraged by two positive reviews, the sisters hastened to mail off their first novels to their publisher. But their optimism was premature; despite early signs of promise, the book of poetry sold a grand total of two copies. Still, Charlotte didn't give up.

The year that finally brought Charlotte into literary triumph and scandal would ultimately be overshadowed by a landscape of total personal devastation. *Jane Eyre* appeared in 1847, but Charlotte could barely devote any time to its growing popularity, the public's obsession with its author's secret identity, and the scathing assessments of its "unchristian" subject matter. As her book took on a life of its own, Charlotte's own life was unraveling. Branwell drank himself to death in 1848. Her eccentric sisters followed soon after, succumbing to tuberculosis within three months of one another. Charlotte and her father were all alone.

Charlotte shielded herself from her pain with the thing that had always gotten her through: writing. "If you think, from this prelude, that anything like a romance is preparing for you, reader, you never were more mistaken," she wrote in the preface to her novel *Shirley* in 1849. "Do you anticipate sentiment, and poetry, and reverie? Do you expect passion, and stimulus, and melodrama? Calm your expectations; reduce them to a lowly standard. Something real, cool and solid lies before you; something unromantic as Monday morning." Though she steadfastly turned herself to the duties that lay ahead, the years that followed her losses were the loneliest and most uncertain she had ever faced. Was this the end of life?

Charlotte's alter ego asks herself the same question in the darkest chapters of *Jane Eyre*, a book that has much to teach us about loyalty and steadfastness. The abandonment, hopelessness, and devastation of Charlotte's personal life pales in comparison with the trials she gave Jane, an impoverished orphan who must make her way through a hostile and immoral world. Just when Jane thinks she has found true love and a peaceful existence, Charlotte snatches the rug from under her feet. Edward Rochester, the moody man Jane loves with her entire life, reveals a disastrous secret at the altar: he is already married. Even worse, his wife is a mad-woman who lives in the attic of the house where the now hopelessly star-crossed couple fell in love.

Here's where it gets good. Anyone who has cracked open *Jane Eyre* is not likely to soon forget the emotional ordeal that follows as Jane faces the love of her life and refuses his request to be her lover, if not her husband.

I was experiencing an ordeal: a hand of fiery iron grasped my vitals. Terrible moment: full of struggle, blackness, burning! Not a human being that ever lived could wish to be loved better than I was loved; and him who thus loved me I absolutely worshipped: and I must renounce love and idol. One drear word com-prised my intolerable duty—"Depart!"

"Jane, you understand what I want of you? Just this promise—'I will be yours, Mr. Rochester.' "

"Mr. Rochester, I will not be yours."

Lashed by the whip of principle, Jane flees across the moors, ending up exhausted, starving, and entirely de-based as she starts a new life of voluntary separation from the only person she has ever loved. Jane is clearly poised for a comeback, but first she must undergo some of the most harrowing chapters in English literature. Charlotte almost revels in Jane's devastation, but she won't let her wallow for long. Slowly, she builds Jane back up, first through blind hope, then through abstract faith, and finally through the deeds and the love of other people.

> A weakness, beginning inwardly, extending to the limbs, seized me, and I fell: I lay on the ground some minutes, pressing my face to the wet turf. I had some fear—or hope—that here I should die: but I was soon up; crawling forwards on my hands and knees, and then again raised to my feet—as eager and as determined as ever to reach the road.

What possible redeeming value can there be in this ultimate of darkest hours before dawn? Fortunately for Jane, and for us, Charlotte has buried a kernel of hope in the storm, and within her heroine. Jane's rebirth is not one of brute persistence or of bravery, though she persists and is brave. It is of internal steadfastness, a dogged adherence to personal principles and values even when she is literally floored by grief and fear.

In the chapters that follow Jane's flight, Charlotte and

Jane get down to the nitty-gritty of what can sustain a person through a personal crisis of epic proportions. Jane the person is stripped down piece by piece, voluntarily turning her back on her relationships, her past associations, and even her name (she goes by a pseudonym in order to escape search and rescue by Rochester). Faced with the crisis of a relationship gone horribly wrong, one that threatens both her place in society and in the eyes of God, Jane refuses to take the easy way out. Instead, she chooses certain misery, shedding that which does not serve her principles. "Life, however," she reflects, "was yet in my possession; with all its requirements, and pains, and responsibilities. The burden must be carried; the want provided for; the suffering endured; the responsibility fulfilled. I set out."

At first, it seems like there won't be much left to set out toward. Jane has consciously dumped the trappings of the beautiful bride and is left only with her plain garb and meager possessions. Jane the social construct—the governess, the unlikely bride, the future Mrs. Rochester—is meaningless out on the moors. All that's left is Jane as she truly is—a lost soul.

Jane's journey through terror, abandonment, and conflicted emotions takes on a nightmarish quality for a while. Her lament echoed by the wild landscape she encounters, she does not stop. Though she has little to be thankful for, she gives thanks. And she keeps walking.

Does Jane's strength come from her utter rootlessness, from the lessons of a life of hardship, toil, and emotional deprivation? Perhaps. But Jane is as human as her creator. As she wanders along in a crisis partly of her own making, strength and weakness seem interchangeable. Faced with a difficulty (and what a difficulty!), Jane has chosen loyalty to herself over loyalty to her love. The hardships of her life have not been enough to soften her. If she stays with Rochester, she will doubtless enjoy the rest of her life . . . and burn in hell for all eternity. So she goes, suffering as much from her self-imposed isolation as from the knowledge that she has wounded the one she holds most dear.

Principles got Jane into this mess, and eventually they get her back out again. Jane's steadfastness endangers her one meager chance at happiness and sets her life on a course of survival and focus. But the act of clinging, the very practice of steadfastness, defines and hones the principles themselves.

Jane's deluge takes away everything she has come to value, but it has something to give in return. That journey is the crucible in which her true character—that of a woman who combines principle with a loving heart, a woman who can't bear mere duty and learns to temper her natural severity with love—is forged. And, tellingly, it is a journey Jane must make alone. All the brooding lovers and abusive teachers in England couldn't teach Jane as much about herself or her core values as a few days wandering the moors, looking for salvation, and searching for the next right step. Though she would be content to fall into the moors and become a part of the outdoors, she does not die. She stands up, moves forward, asks for help. Ultimately, Jane makes her way back to Rochester and finds her happy ending. Steadfastness rewarded, she survives.

Charlotte, too, clung steadfastly to life over death. After a period of intense grief, she entered the world of English literary lights on her own terms, ventured out from Haworth and brushed shoulders with London high society. She even married, leaving behind the spinsterhood that defined and confined much of her adult life. Though fated to die young (she succumbed to dehydration in 1855 following a bout of uncontrollable morning sickness after only a few months of marriage), Charlotte had one thing in common with her plain Jane: she couldn't be beaten by life.

Any heroine worth reading about will one day find herself on the moors of a devastating personal crisis. For the most part, we must traverse them alone. We would do well to remember Charlotte and Jane as we come face to face with our inadequacy and our inner strength.

The moment of crossing is one of isolation, humility, and despair. But as heroines, we are already equipped with everything we need. Inside every heroine is the lovelorn, lonely writer who kept on working; the plain governess who kept on walking toward her principles. Even when we're too scared to function or too grief-stricken to care, we can be carried along by steadfast actions like Jane's. Our steadfastness punctures the fear and isolation of the deluge, enabling us to address only that which deserves our attention and keep putting one foot in front of the other, bad reviews and broken hearts notwithstanding.

I first encountered *Jane Eyre* when I was far too young to understand the sweep of its great love story and its great tale of cleaving to one's self as steadfastly as to any other love. I loved it then for what it gave me, but I love it more now for what I bring to every reading. It's a book I revisit again and again: when I seek to see myself amid the threat of depression and feeble people-pleasing, when I need to bolster myself for storms of my own making. Every time, it's a bit different, some parts familiar and soothing, others jarring and rude. But every time I finish *Jane Eyre*, I marvel at how plain and poor Jane can adhere so unbreakably to her own truth. This steadfastness pushes her into heroic territory, even when it seems as if she will come out with nothing but her principles. It's the thing that carries her through one of literature's more turbulent love stories without separating her from herself or her ideals.

Like Jane, we are goaded by peril and stress, loss and unimaginable redefinition. First, we lose sight of ourselves. Then we hone in, regroup. Suddenly, clarity sets in: unimportant things are shelved until later; our selves are identified, then cared for. Slowly, painfully, we become even more loyal to that which we know to be right. We stand up. We ask for help, even when doing so seems "as unromantic as Monday morning." We walk on toward ourselves. And we make our way forward, as long as we don't cling too tightly to the principles that drive us onward. Like Jane Eyre and Charlotte Brontë, we find we "must struggle on, strive to live and bend to toil like the rest."

READ THIS BOOK:

- In the midst of breakups and life passages
- With a box of tissues at hand
- When you're not sure if you can deal with another personal bombshell

JANE'S LITERARY SISTERS:

- Mrs. de Winter in *Rebecca*, by Daphne du Maurier
- Cassandra Mortmain in *I Capture the Castle*, by
  Dodie Smith
- Cathy Earnshaw in *Wuthering Heights*, by Emily
  Brontë

CHAPTER 11

AMBITION

Jo March in *Little Women*, by Louisa May Alcott

Any mention of her "works" always had a bad effect upon Jo, who either grew rigid and looked offended, or changed the subject with a brusque remark, as now. "Sorry you could find nothing better to read. I write that rubbish because it sells, and ordinary people like it."

LOUISA MAY ALCOTT, *LITTLE WOMEN*

Louisa May Alcott had always imagined her return from her first trip to Europe as a kind of triumph, a graceful homecoming replete with happy memories and artistic and romantic accomplishments aplenty. The reality was somewhat different: fourteen nauseous, boring days aboard the *Africa* led not to fanfare and tearful reunions but to the damp, anticlimactic feeling that overcame her as she looked out over the Boston harbor that meant home. The Europe of her childhood fantasies had been something to energize, inspire, and satisfy; the one she had just seen had turned her into an invalid nearly as cranky as the one she had been sent to supervise.

As a companion to Anna Weld, the thirty-three-year-old had seen Switzerland, London, Paris. But her obligations to her nervous, frivolous charge had kept her from wandering or exploring on her own, a fact she resented more with every passing day. Miss Weld didn't care about the scenery that surrounded her, and her neurotic chatter drove Louisa nearly mad with boredom and anger. Neither new friends nor unfamiliar sights could undo the fact that here, too, was unrelenting work, her constant companion since childhood. Even the sudden gift of money from her mother was just a stopgap measure. While it allowed her to spend a few brief weeks luxuriating in London, she knew she was operating on borrowed time. Characteristically, she was also doing so on borrowed money. When she came home, listless and sick, she realized that the gift had been lent by well-meaning friends. Guilty and angry, she went through the family finances, falling back into her old role of problem-solver and reluctant breadwinner.

It was in this fretful state of mind, compounded by the recent death of her beloved brother-in-law, that Louisa received her publisher's commission—and it was an unusual one. She'd made her career first as an anonymous writer of lurid serials, then as author of a wildly popular book drawing on her experiences as a nurse in the Civil War. To her surprise, publisher Thomas Niles wanted neither— he wanted a book for girls. Louisa herself was an unmarried tomboy who knew little about children, let alone little women. She was also poor. "Niles asked me to write a girls book. . . . Fuller asked me to be the editor of [popular children's magazine] *Merry's Museum*. Said I'd try," she wrote in her journal. "Began at once on both jobs, but didn't like either."

That statement about sums up Louisa's complex relationship to the only constants in her life: work and ambition. What we today associate with clocking in, sitting in meetings, or standing behind a counter meant something very different in the 1840s, when Louisa was a girl. To the Alcott sisters, "work" was the backbreaking labor expected of a woman, shorthand for the hours of sewing, mending, fitting, and patterning a girl had to perform simply to have clothing to wear in a world that lacked washing machines, detergent, or ready-made anything. "Work" was scrubbing a blackened hearth, kneading bread, lugging heavy buckets of water into the house from an outdoor well. For Louisa, this drudgery distracted from her true ambitions, desires born as much from deprivation as dreams.

When the family moved to Fruitlands, a utopian community in Harvard, Massachusetts, in 1843, their workload only increased. The community was the brainchild of Louisa's father, Bronson, and his deluded apostles, men with an insatiable, albeit impractical, need to put their lofty philosophies into action. When they moved to the rocky farm, the "consociate" family took a vow never to use any product of an animal's life or toil, be it wool, silk, or fields plowed by horses. Louisa and her siblings starved together on sour apples (potatoes and other root vegetables were off-limits due to their "toxic" downward-pointing tendencies) and watched their parents' marriage nearly fail, unable to withstand suggestions of celibacy or wife-sharing. Over the course of that dreary year, Louisa and her sisters watched their father reduced to a shell of his former self, a man even more unfit for honest labor than he had been in the early days when he wandered the country as a peddler of household goods, living on the kindness of strangers and the less-than-edible fruits of his complex philosophical tenets.

In those days, a father unable or unwilling to provide

for his family exposed them to the very real prospect of illness, imprisonment, and starvation. Abba Alcott and her girls had long lived side by side with debt and dependence; they'd relied on family members and the charity of Bronson's more stable Transcendentalist friends. Now they themselves had to go out to work, taking on positions as teachers, governesses, and social workers.

Herself the prisoner of complex ambitions and overwhelming insecurities, Louisa longed to prove herself. She had already tried and failed to sell her sewing and her stories; now, despite her mother's misgivings, she agreed to work as a maid in the home of James Richardson, a family friend. Eager to see something, anything, of the world, she arrived at the Richardson house ready to earn a living.

The position was a bit more than she had bargained for; in addition to her stated work, she was apparently expected to act as a sort of paid girlfriend to Richardson, who regaled her with long philosophical ramblings and sexually harassed her. When she objected, her language tart and charged with anger, she paid the price. Her new tasks included shoveling snow and withstanding the abusive notes Richardson shoved under her door. She drew the line at blacking her inappropriate employer's boots, fleeing at the first possible opportunity. In exchange for two months of boring, humiliating, and unsatisfying labor, she was paid just four dollars. She sent the money back, traumatized and embittered by her first real experience working outside the home.

From then on she teeter-tottered between pride in her efforts and hatred for work itself. The ugly realities of a woman's work were sometimes offset by her anxiety to make something of herself. But the women she saw all around her never got that opportunity. Ultimately measured by their ability to marry well, the women in Louisa's life were limited to "ladylike" pursuits that were inevitably lowly and poorly paid. Sewing and tutoring, cleaning and governessing, were like torture for Louisa, who grew into a gangly, twitchy young woman with a decided lack of good grace. She knew she was a disappointment. Though she was the natural helpmeet of her industrious but harried mother, her headstrong and passionate nature had always confused Bronson, who wrote judgmental notes in her journals and publicly decried his daughter's untamed willfulness. Unlike her sisters, Louisa could not check her impulsive temper, her tomboyish nature, or her inner critic. Uncertain of her place in her family, she buried herself in books and writing.

When the Civil War began in 1861, it both reflected and spurred on Louisa's directionless anger, dejection, and angst. She was still mourning the dual loss of one sister to scarlet fever and another to marriage when the idea came to her: perhaps a woman could go to war. Motivated by her thirtieth birthday and a surge of patriotic fervor, she volunteered as a nurse at the Union Hotel Hospital in Washington. Work had a different meaning altogether in the hospital's bloody halls. Surrounded by the chaos of death and battle, she drowned her own worries in merciful acts, neglecting her own health even as she dressed others' wounds. But her strong constitution was no match for the typhoid epidemic that swept through the hospital like a forest fire. Soon the nurse was a patient herself, engulfed in delirium and dosed with calomel, a mercury compound used to treat the fatal fever. She was too feeble to protest when Bronson arrived unexpectedly to take her home.

As she struggled through a slow recovery, she realized that her nursing experience had resulted in nothing but poverty and bitterness. Weak and listless, she turned inward again, struggling to make sense of what she had seen through writing. Dramatic Louisa had always thrown herself into her work with an almost Byronic passion, and writing was no exception. After months of dormancy, she would let a writing "vortex" take over, sucking her down and in until she was preoccupied and unfit for mannered conversation of any kind. Armed with her pen, she angrily denied her family access to her quarters, writing day and night until completely drained and depleted. She rested, socialized, then did it again, repeating the cycle until she had a piece of salable writing that she swiftly translated into a carpet for her mother's sitting room or a bonnet for her sister. She had no way of knowing that her stint at the hospital would forever deprive her of her health. Bent over her work, she was barely strong enough to survive the physical pain that accompanied every vortex.

It's unsettling to realize that it's in this state of mind—anxious, overworked, unhealthy, and tired—that Louisa set out to write a story so familiar it's as if it were written by a family member. It's even worse to acknowledge that *Little Women*—the stuff of movies and musicals, the book that's never been out of print—was written for money and money alone. I'd much rather envision a scribbling Jo, transported by passion and pain, hurrying to eulogize her perfect childhood and pass its greatness on to other generations. Instead, reality presents me with Louisa, cranky and well dosed with morphine and opium, bent over work she neither valued nor enjoyed. Still, the net effect is the same—under pressure to produce, Louisa turned to her childhood and her own turbulent personality and gave us Jo March, a heroine who, like her creator, has plenty of work to do.

It's almost unthinkable that a woman as spirited and funny as tomboyish Jo would be a de facto outcast in her time, someone to be subdued and suppressed. But in a world of matching gloves and strict codes of womanhood, Jo's a worrisome anomaly. Proper girls sit up straight and are silent; Jo stretches out on carpets, singes dresses, and loses her hairpins running down hills. Real women work without a word of complaint. But while there is substantial work for Jo to do—she must sew all of her own clothing, help with the household chores, and serve as a companion to her crotchety Aunt March—she complains lustily while doing it. At the heart of Jo's protest is overwork: can't she be a carefree girl a little while longer? At the same time, she objects to the inanity of needle-pushing and primping when all around her there is *real* work to be done, the work of war and substantial wages, the work of the men who are almost entirely absent from the book. It's frustrating to see Jo bashing up against her own ambitions with no outlet, no hope of progress, nothing but the kindliness of her family and friends to sustain her. But what a way to appreciate the freedoms we are given a century later!

Myself a feminist as staunch as Louisa, I can't help but wonder if my affection for *Little Women*, with its self-sacrificing daughters and tongue-holding mothers, should go the way of the hoop skirt. Still, I can't help loving mercurial Jo, revisiting the book to see how Louisa challenges the expectations that drip from every seam of her own beloved story. Externally, *Little Women* seeks to instill all of the boring values of boxed-in femininity on its readers. Pickled limes and vanity: bad! Self-abnegation and backbreaking labor: good! The need for self-denial is impressed on Jo and her sisters at every turn; instead of setting aside your dishpans and going for a hike in the woods, you should stay at home where you are needed. Cheerful Beth, who goes about her housework with a song on her lips, is a saint; Jo, with her complaints and her awkwardness and her inability to cook, is a dangerous hoyden.

But look again. Once you drop the desire to see suppression in every page, it's easy to find Jo's rebellion. In a move that's outraged readers since 1869, she refuses to marry Laurie, a young man with the advantages of being dashing, rich, hotheaded, and adoring. But Jo isn't ready to lay down her arms and take up her needle (or put on a wedding ring) just yet. By refusing to indulge her best friend, she is a better friend to herself, a self in need of air and freedom, the liberty she'd never possess in the expensive trappings of a Mrs. Laurence. Though she cries when she sells her luxurious hair to help her mother reach her wounded

father, it's something she abandons with an eye toward un-
encumbered movement. In the past, I always thought of
these gutsy moves as idiosyncratic ones, little quirks designed to make me say, "Oh, Jo!" and smile and get back
to my self-denial. But when I really read the words, I realize that these small moves of mutiny go far beyond en-
dearing personality traits. In Jo, Louisa unwittingly (or,
even better, purposely) unmasks her little outlets, the very
things she relied on to drag herself through a life of crushing expectation and ugly, unremitting labor.

In one of my favorite passages of the book, Jo is, at last,
"All Alone." Every other member of the March family is
occupied: Meg with her unruly babies, Beth with the angels
in a heaven doubtless spackled with kittens and ugly dolls,
Amy in Europe on the very cross-continental trip that's
been denied her harum-scarum sister. For the first time in
her life, Jo's at a real loss. She looks around and sees a life
of endless toil:

> Something like despair came over her when she
> thought of spending all her life in that quiet house,
> devoted to humdrum cares, a few poor little plea-
> sures, and the duty that never seemed to grow any
> easier.

These passages are not-so-shockingly similar to Louisa's own angsty letter to her sister a few years before:

> If I think of my woes I fall into a vortex of debts, dish pans, and despondency awful to see. . . . All very aggravating to a young woman with one dollar, no bonnet, half a gown, and a discontented mind. It's a mercy the mountains are everlasting, for it will be a century before *I* get there. Oh, me, such is life!

The expression of Louisa's despair through Jo might seem like a mere narrative device, but there's that outlet again. It took guts to declare your dissatisfaction with life in the 1860s, in a day and age where women's wrongs were not just ignored, but actively stifled. And it feels good to see the sloppy, ungovernable emotion beneath Louisa's self-proclaimed hack job.

Better yet is the delicious vent Louisa gives her own heroine. Like her creator, Jo must act when mired in the slough of despond; like Louisa, she writes her way out of every hole. Discontented with her feeble options and frustrated with her own ennui, she goes up to the attic, readjusts her ridiculous writing cap, and gets to work. Here is the true apex of Louisa's literary rebellion: unlike her creator, Jo is allowed literary success writing books she loves. Her stint writing pulp has been unprofitable and left her numb; as it was for Louisa, the creative work she performs from a place of insecurity or lack is bound to be unsuccessful. Jo writes for herself, out of her own experience, and the truth that comes from that heroine's self gives her the success Louisa chased her entire life.

I would rather write that Jo's literary triumph mirrors her creator's, but in reality they were different creatures indeed. *Little Women* itself was a literary sensation, but it came at an awful price. "Paid up all the debts, praise the Lord!" wrote Louisa after completing the book. "Now I feel as if I could die in peace." But shouts of happiness over her new financial freedom were undercut by worry that her work would never be taken seriously. The ambition that drove her literary success prevented her from devoting herself to the adult novels she longed to write.

Angry with a public who disturbed her privacy and demanded constant access to their favorite literary celebrity, Louisa struggled vainly against her new role. Unable to take herself seriously, the girl her father had called "duty's faithful child" did the only thing she knew how to do: she worked, hard, cranking out stories of placid childhoods and good little women long after there was a financial need.

Her nervous system was so used to deprivation and want that she never really learned how to enjoy her fame or her money. She could not have known that she was already dying. Louisa herself thought that the cure to the typhoid she had contracted during her nursing days had brought mercury poisoning along with it; present-day scholars suspect she suffered from lupus. Either way, the work that plagued her, obsessed her, and even killed her was also her literary gift to us.

It's hard to imagine a heroine more companionable than Jo March, a young woman whose attitude toward work was somewhat more balanced than her creator's. In the 1860s, her power was as an alternative to the buttoned-down, boring girl who followed all rules and mastered self-sacrifice. That girl has long since faded from fashion, but Jo remains as a tantalizing option, the opposite of fear and insecurity, inaction and perfection. Jo is an Erin Brockovich in a world of corporate sheep, a Christiane Amanpour in a land of pseudo-journalists, an alternative to mundane, muted reality. When Jo works, she does so from a sense of duty, a knowledge that the bills must be paid while Father is off at the war. But she also eventually works from a place of pleasure, tackling projects that are self-supporting and self-defined. Hardworking Jo never shies away from a challenge, and her success gives us something Louisa May Alcott craved but never attained: the possibility of a life in which ambition firmly occupies its proper place.

A workaholic myself, I have much to learn from a heroine who divides her most tedious sewing into hemispheres and talks about geography as she sews. I could do worse than turn my daily struggles into a Pilgrim's Progress like the March girls. As heroines, we inherit our foremothers' less appealing traits and trials: a tendency to overwork, off-kilter time management skills, and the never-ending challenge of bringing our work in line with the rest of our lives. Ambition is a heroine's trait only when it adds to life instead of detracting from it. Louisa would be proud and happy to see that a modern woman can choose any avenue for her life's work, that our road is easier than the one she trod so resolutely and so ruefully. But fewer obstacles doesn't mean fewer obligations. Though we have it relatively easy, we still face the challenges of being taken seriously, of proving that our efforts have some meaning and worth. It takes guts to show up for life, to tackle what we are handed. And it takes even more strength and courage not to confuse self-sacrifice with self-sustenance.

A heroine's work—growth, self-definition, barrier-smashing—is never really done. Let us heed Louisa's warning and do as Jo does, taking up the work that's right for us instead of that which we feel obligated to pursue, work that consistently creates the independence Louisa sought when she wrote, "I think I shall come out right, and prove that though an Alcott I *can* support myself. I like the independent feeling [of working], and though not an easy life, it is a free one, and I enjoy it . . . I will make a battering-ram of my head and make a way through this rough-and-tumble world."

READ THIS BOOK:

- After a fight with a family member or daughter
- When you're ready to walk out on your job
- On days when you'd rather sell your hair than get out of bed

JO'S LITERARY SISTERS:

- Esther Greenwood in *The Bell Jar*, by Sylvia Plath
- Frankie Landau-Banks in *The Disreputable History of Frankie Landau-Banks*, by E. Lockhart
- Lucy Snowe in *Villette*, by Charlotte Brontë

CHAPTER 12

MAGIC

Mary Lennox in *The Secret Garden*, by Frances Hodgson Burnett

"Somehow, something always happens," she cried, "just before things get to the very worst. It is as if the Magic did it. If I could only just remember that always. The worst thing never QUITE comes."

FRANCES HODGSON BURNETT, *A LITTLE PRINCESS*

Frances Hodgson Burnett hadn't aged well. Gossip had always been her closest companion, but it seemed to finally have taken its toll. Now the worst had come: not only was she a laughingstock, but her florid, romantic writing style, the words that had made her a star, had gone out of vogue. She had tried to stay relevant, penning books with toxic undercurrents of rape, scandal, and physical abuse instead of the flowery stories for children that had sealed her fame, but her efforts had done nothing to revive her literary reputation. Alone in her garden in 1910, she had plenty of time to think things over.

Solitude used to be a blessing. It was in solitude that she discovered the seedy and the beautiful side of Manchester, England, the city in which she was a little girl, blissfully unaware of her family's rapid slide into poverty and obscurity. It was in solitude that she discovered the wilds of the countryside around Knoxville, Tennessee, where she moved with her mother and siblings in search of a better life away from Manchester's dying economy, which had been ravaged by the decline of cotton production due to the American Civil War. A lonely teenager, Frances picked wild grapes in the woods, selling the fruit and using the proceeds to buy paper for the writing she had already discovered could bring in infinitesimal sums to help support her family. Back then, she feared she would never be successful: her surroundings were simply too plain and fortune too far away to grasp. "What is there to feed my poor, little, busy brain in this useless, weary, threadbare life? I can't eat my own heart forever," she wrote fretfully to a suitor. "I can't write things that are worth reading if I never see things which are worth seeing, or speak to people who are worth hearing. I cannot weave silk if I see nothing but calico—calico—calico."

The calico years stretched into a decade, and Frances, who described herself as "a pen-driving machine," knew that writing was her only hope. She staunchly ignored the repeated proposals of her Knoxville neighbor, Swan Burnett, returning briefly to England in pursuit of glamour and success. On her return, she finally gave in to Swan's steadfast courtship, agreeing to accompany him to Paris as he pursued studies in his specialty, eye and ear medicine. The newlyweds were poor, but as Frances continued to write, their fortunes improved steadily. By the time her breakthrough novel, *That Lass o' Lowrie's*, appeared in 1877, she'd been supporting Swan for years. What began as a financial exigency became a sort of dirty secret between the couple, both of whom were ashamed and frustrated by Swan's inability to support his own even after they settled in Washington, D.C.

Frances had long forgotten her calico by the time her little sons came along, breaking the solitude she felt under the surface of her outwardly successful marriage. Her treatment of them provoked a minor scandal in itself when she allowed them to sleep at her feet while she wrote her best sellers, giving rise to ugly talk when it was revealed that they dug in her expansive gardens using her finest silver. They were her best friends, her confidants, her literary inspiration for books like *Little Lord Fauntleroy*, that sentimental tale dripping with idealization of Victorian youth.

But motherhood, as revered as it was in Victorian society, was not enough to shade Frances from unsavory accusations. She may have been a mother, but she was one who smoked cigarettes and indulged in expensive, opulent art and clothing. At first she was a glamorous enigma, but her growing fame meant growing scrutiny. Her frivolous dress and love of society earned her the slightly mocking nickname "Fluffy," a moniker she took in stride, even adopting the name in her correspondence. Though she had plenty of time for balls, at-homes, and parties, Frances kept to a brutal work schedule, often appearing at social functions peaked and exhausted. The gossips were intrigued. She was clearly unhappy in her marriage, and for a while stifled, bored wives were stock characters in her popular novels. And why did she work so hard, anyway? Couldn't her husband pay the bills?

Truth be told, she had supported Swan for so long that she knew no other way. Yes, it was unconventional for a woman to be the family breadwinner, but she saw no reason to stop once the money really appeared. Her exhaustion pointed to a deeper problem, an addiction to self-sacrifice and stress. Finally she collapsed, taking a three-year sabbatical from writing and devoting herself to her sons.

The years that followed bore little resemblance to anything but her most sordid tales. Unable to risk the fallout of a divorce, Frances soldiered on in an untenable relationship, the constant nagging of the publicity hounds who followed her every move making a bad marriage even worse. The rumors were incessant, but so were her own infidelities, some of which kept her away from the United States for long periods of time. She was overseas with Stephen Townesend, a much younger man, when she got news that her son Lionel had a mild case of influenza.

Herself struggling to recover from a riding accident that had left her in a coma for several days, Frances had no way of knowing that her son's illness was severe. It is unclear when she realized that Lionel was dying, but she did not hurry to his bedside. Her erratic visits were punctuated by liaisons with Stephen and long absences that involved giving away toys at children's charity events in her ailing son's name. Finally, she returned to Lionel. She took him overseas, seeking relief at sanatoriums across Europe, but to no avail. The sixteen-year-old died of tuberculosis in December 1890.

Still devastated six years after Lionel's death, Frances finally found the strength to do what she had feared for years. But her 1898 divorce only created more marital troubles. Stephen transformed from ardent lover to angry man, finally blackmailing her into a marriage marred by angry episodes that seemed to be related to Stephen's bipolar illness. "He talks about 'my duties as a wife,' " wrote an angry Frances, "as if I had married him of my own accord—as if I had not been forced and blackguarded and blackmailed into it." Frustrated by the bad press surrounding her attachment to a much younger man, Frances protested, then resigned herself to paying him to stay away from her until their divorce two years later. Had it really come to this?

Frances's own childhood story was full of enchantment, of odds and tatters, and finally, of riches. The tales this childhood had inspired gained her acclaim and money. Now, weathered with years of hardship and strain, she looked back onto that little girl in a new light, squinting hard to see the woman inside who was more than frivolous "Fluffy." Despite everything, she was still unabashedly romantic and guardedly optimistic. She was a woman who believed in vague spirits and mysticism in the face of the loss of everything she held dear. Looking inside, Frances began to write.

She had always found solace in the outdoors, and her garden became her greatest comfort. Surrounded by her books, her grandchildren, and the unorthodox spirituality she had dabbled in since her son's death, she knew it was time to rest. Finally free from the years of self-sacrifice and toil, the constant pressure to conjure up money and prestige out of thin air with that pen of hers, she had a moment to breathe in and out again. And then she did what she always did. She started writing, devoting herself to another children's story. But this time it was different. This time, she had magic on her side.

Any girl who has snapped sourly at her parents or scowled at well-meaning friends won't just identify with the loathsome, dour heroine of *The Secret Garden*—she will love her. Mary Lennox is ugly and unlovable, cranky and sour, the polar opposite of adorable, long-locked Lord Fauntleroy and of Sara Crewe, whom fortune always favors. No, Mary is one of literature's least appealing heroines, in the great vein of her literary sisters like Jane Eyre and Jo March. Mary's not just contrary—she's entirely out of her element. A child of imperialist India, she is left to her own devices in an unfamiliar country and surrounded by unknown faces.

Mary is not a favorable candidate for transplantation of any kind. She longs for companionship but fears it, wilting in her uncle's locked-up house and unable to adjust to servants who don't do as she bids them, food that doesn't taste as it ought, and a climate that's the polar opposite of the Indian heat in which she was raised. She seems poised to curl up and die in the interminable English winter that chilled this California girl to the bone every time I picked up *The Secret Garden* for a glimpse into Mary's fate. And yet there are glimpses of motion in hibernating Mary: a jump rope, a friendly chambermaid, a tantalizing mystery just outside Misselthwaite Manor. The minute that Mary is led to her titular garden by a little bird, we know that she'll do just fine.

The details of *The Secret Garden* are as familiar as a daisy, which makes it all the more shocking to read through adult eyes. By the time I picked up the book as a child, I was used to the idea of orphaned, imprisoned, and unloved girls (and liked to fancy I was one myself). But I wasn't able to appreciate the cruelty and despair of Mary's isolation until I reread the book as a grown-up very attuned to the little girl I once was. Mary can't grow in a vacuum, and she can't get started at all until she has a place of her own.

The Secret Garden is a gardener's success story: the spare little cutting, attractive to no one and never one to thrive, does eventually bud. At first it seems unlikely she'll ever manage. Disenfranchised, she is little and lonely, separated from her people and her place of origin. Her family is gone, and so is India, and Mary is tight and restricted within the confines of her ugly, jaundiced bulb. Slowly, though, magic happens. The sour, sallow child warms and relaxes, grows and stretches until she's in bloom, too, in the midst of a garden all her own.

Yes, Mary grows, and having a place of her own is part of the equation. The garden, that "bit of earth" she is granted so grudgingly, is to be her new home for now. Left for dead so many years ago, the garden becomes a center, first for the children who play there, then for a family reunion as intense as the romance that once closed it off. Secure in the bit of earth she has managed to clear inside herself, Mary is finally ready to let others in, starting with cousin Colin. A kind of reverse Bertha Rochester, Colin is a child who is as irritating as he is sickly, and pouty Mary seems tailor-made to rock his tiny, whiny world. But who would think that Mary of all people could bring a bit of magic to Misselthwaite?

Over the course of the book, Mary begins to use the word *magic* more and more, until it becomes a sort of short-hand for all that is great and beautiful. It's not necessarily spiritual; it's something you can reach out and touch. It's a crocus pushing its way out of the ground, a cranky child becoming playful and generous, a gift of simple food enjoyed among friends, a father's pride in his son. It also works on a grander scale, for Mary and for us, stopping us all in our tracks as we realize that a world of death, asphyxiation, and isolation has been turned into one full of light, air, health, and love. These qualities were all inherent in the dead, lonely garden itself; they were inside Mary, too, though if left to her own devices she might never have discovered them.

What Mary comes to see as Magic, capital *M*, is found in ordinary things: learning to love herself and others, seeing herself in a gentler and more flattering light. But magic is also nature, the things that sustain us but are bigger and more powerful than us. Magic is inside Colin's wobbly, wizened legs and Mary's reddening cheeks. It's inside the whole world of breathless bees and climbing vines contained inside the secret garden's walls. And, Frances insists, it is inside, too:

> "Of course there must be lots of Magic in the world . . . but people don't know what it is like or how to make it. Perhaps the beginning is just to say nice things are going to happen until you make them happen."

I don't know about you, but I find the thought that we get to conjure our own magic to be a comforting one. Mary's garden could never grow if she herself didn't discover and believe in it. And we can't possibly expand beyond ourselves if we don't discover and trust that which we find within.

In one of the book's most compelling scenes, colicky Colin, the child of "I can't," is so infuriated by the suggestion that his feeble legs are crooked that he stands in defiant anger. Energized by his belief in himself and the care and compassion he has received from others for the first time, he moves into a world of potential and possibility. Unsure he can, he does anyway . . . and we are led to believe that Mary's own will and recognition of the power within this ugly child is part of the equation.

"Are you making Magic?" he asked sharply.

Dickon's curly mouth spread in a cheerful grin.

"Tha's doin' Magic thysel'," he said. "It's same Magic as made these 'ere work out o' th' earth," and he touched with his thick boot a clump of crocuses in the grass. . . . He heard Mary muttering something under her breath. . . . But she did not tell him [what she said]. What she was saying was this:

"You can do it! You can do it! I told you you could!
You can do it! You can do it! You *can*!"

Yes, heroines can make their own magic when they
expect the highest and best of themselves and others. Magic
summons up all of our secrets, turning them upside-down
like old roots in fresh earth, uprooting the pain and isolation of an ugly, oppressed childhood and making it whole
and good again in the light of day. Magic draws the sun up
from its bed, calms anxiety, powers the insides of people
who were shriveled, ugly, and small before their time. It
embodies all the risk and potential of daily life, cyclical
and obscure, a life that can and does mean something if we
are brave enough to grow beyond ourselves. Magic occurs
when, like Mary, we love others despite our deepest misgivings, pushing our boundaries even when, as for Frances, the world only offers us hurt and betrayal in return.

When I reread *The Secret Garden*, I hear echoes of the
mockery Frances Hodgson Burnett endured for her ideal-
ism and her frivolity, her insistence on avoiding newspapers and the sad stories they contained. But to dismiss her,
or her work, as unfashionable is shortsighted indeed. It's
the equivalent of dismissing ourselves during those awkward, ugly years, the years in which we had no idea of our

own potential or our own futures. Whoever would think that Frances's most enduring book would be among her last, the product in part of stress, despair, and heartbreak? To underestimate her would have been to deny a magical book.

Times of crisis usually mean that practical thinking trumps childish woes, crowding out magic as we return to grim reality. It's hard to admit that we're childish inside. We may turn back to girlish books like *The Secret Garden*, but we often do so in secret. After all, haven't we been taught that we have to not only survive but master our unrelentingly adult world? No matter how successful or mature I become, I carry a smaller version of myself inside, and that spazzy, dramatic girl is always twitching for attention and for love. Too often as adults, as heroines who have seen their share of crises and chaos, we're tempted to turn our eyes away from the smaller selves within. We're taught to focus on what's ahead; an admirable tactic, and one that can serve us well. But when we lose sense of that child, of the magic in our lives and inner landscapes, we risk losing the force that connects us irreparably to ourselves, to nature, to mystery, and to one another.

Frances Hodgson Burnett spoke up for the unappealing, peevish children among us, the ones who didn't take well to the customs of school or public gatherings, the ones, like me, for whom curbing the emotions was a lesson learned late, if at all. Born of familiar concerns—sadness, isolation, overwork—her magical philosophy transcended a career on a downward trajectory and a personal life in shambles. In a story all too familiar to anyone who's borne witness to the downfall of the Lindsay Lohans and Amy Winehouses of our day, her road from calico to literary superstardom gave her even further to fall. But unlike Britney Spears, Frances had a bit of magic to cushion her collapse.

Sometimes, mired in the unbalanced bank account and the lost job and the infuriating relationship and the dying relative, we get stuck in what's in front of us, held captive by our own limited perspective and hard up to achieve even fumbling grace. Faced with heroines' struggles, cholera, and freezing winters, sometimes all we can see through our adult eyes is an impenetrable wall with no door and no key. As adults in a grown-up world, we can choose to see what is in front of us or what could be all around us. We can ask what our favorite author would do, what would make the little girls we once were prouder, bigger, better. We can remember the women who came before us and the heroines they gave us. Bolstered by the stories and the strengths of women real and fictitious, we can bring a child's eyes to the sight of the impossible. We can expect to see magic. Heroines and women all, we just might make some of our own.

READ THIS BOOK:

- When your stomach hurts, and grown-up remedies like ginger tea aren't helping
- In a literary double feature with *A Little Princess*
- When you're feeling contrary

MARY'S LITERARY SISTERS:

- Leslie Burke in *Bridge to Terabithia*, by Katherine Paterson
- Gemma Doyle in *A Great and Terrible Beauty*, by Libba Bray
- Sara Crewe in *A Little Princess*, by Frances Hodgson Burnett

EPILOGUE

In 1863 Louisa May Alcott, bedridden with typhoid after her ill-fated stint as a Civil War nurse, had a strange hallucination. She lay in her bed, sweating and moaning, trying and failing to look away from the dark Spaniard who claimed to be her husband, a man who hid behind curtains and closet doors and took her by surprise again and again. She cried out in agony; he responded with a terrifying "Lie still, my dear."

One hundred and forty-six years later, I lay in my own bed, stricken with my third case of bronchitis in a year. I was nearing the end of the writing process on the book you have just read. Appropriately, through my codeine- and cough-syrup-induced haze, I hallucinated about Louisa herself, imagining her standing in my doorway, her hair trailing down her back like Jo March. But Louisa didn't tell me to lie still. Instead, she admonished me: "Get back to work."

Tired but driven, goaded by a deadline Louisa would have appreciated and a frantic desire to type "The End," I finished the book at last. As I turned off the computer, exhausted, I had another vision, this one uncomfortable but somehow empowering. "My" authors stood in a long row next to their heroines, looking at me in silence across the emptiness of many years. They seemed to want something. Had I met their expectations?

Healthy once more, I'm inclined to conclude that the women of the past don't so much expect something of me as ask me to acknowledge what they have given me. As time weathers the pages of history books, writers like Jane Austen and Zora Neale Hurston move ever further from our grasp. All that's left of these women is what they chose—what they dared—to leave us. In a way, they've burdened us with an extraordinary task: to bring our own life experiences and interpretations to the reading of their lives, their heroines; to keep their legacies alive long after their deaths. To me, the power of these authors lies not just in the books they wrote, but in the lives they led, lives that somehow manage to puncture the distance of continents and centuries.

This realization—this appreciation of the lives of my literary heroines—has been uneasily mirrored in my own writing process, which has challenged my expectations, assumptions, and limits along the way. During the course of writing this book, my own life was disrupted, first by illness and daily woes, then by the death of my beloved grandfather Gerald Kendall Alexander. As I watched my family struggle with an irreplaceable loss, I was reminded of my life's own heroines. I saw my mother, sister, aunts, cousins, and grandmother confront their loss with purpose, self, and dignity . . . qualities that mirror the literary heroines who have done so much to shape me.

As I reflect on lives so heroically lived, I'm reminded that it's a bit too easy to watch a beloved book slip out of print, to forget someone who can never be replaced. By passing on the legacies of the people we love—heroines and relatives and selves alike—we acknowledge their worth and their influence. We're the ones tasked with the survival, the recognition, of the people and things we love. We can lie still, or we can consult our bookshelf and get back to a heroine's work.

ACKNOWLEDGMENTS

Back in headier teenage days, I made a bold pact. I'd dedicate my first book to my friend Richard, and he'd take me to the Oscars when he became a world-renowned director. Years and careers later, I haven't forgotten my promise. First and foremost, this book is dedicated to my surrogate brother and my best friend—not just because I promised, but because of everything he's meant to me over the last twenty-two years.

The book you've just read simply wouldn't exist if it weren't for the patience and endless confidence of my agent, Larry Weissman, and book-obsessed Sascha Alper. I owe them, my editor, Jeanette Perez, copy editor Miranda Ottewell, and everyone at HarperCollins a real debt of gratitude. Thanks also to my beta readers Kyla, Stephanie, Courtney, and Wendy for their invaluable feedback on the first draft of the book.

I'm not sure who I'd be without Kyla, Kathryn, Juli,

Scott, Kj, Nicole, Carol, Olivia, and especially Mike, who have been nothing less than heroic in their unwavering support of me and my writing, as have the countless mentors, friends, and family members who encouraged me every step of the way.